Silver Express

No one needed to tell Sheriff Alec Lawson that thousands of dollars in silver bullion had been stolen from a train on the Northern Colorado Railroad: he was on the train at the time. Now he and his deputies had to search the mountains and mining camps for the thieves.

The more he looked into the robbery, the more Lawson was convinced that it was not just a simple theft. The desire for money was at the root of it all: bribes, bounties, social status and death.

The sheriff and his men were risking their lives for other people's money, and death seems very close when you're riding on the roof of a runaway train!

Silver Express

GILLIAN F. TAYLOR

A Black Horse Western

ROBERT HALE · LONDON

© Gillian F. Taylor 2009
First published in Great Britain 2009

ISBN 978-0-7090-8781-6

Robert Hale Limited
Clerkenwell House
Clerkenwell Green
London EC1R 0HT

www.halebooks.com

Typeset by
Derek Doyle & Associates, Shaw Heath
Printed and bound in Great Britain by
CPI Antony Rowe, Chippenham and Eastbourne

CHAPTER ONE

The train braked unexpectedly, jolting the passengers in their seats. Alec Lawson put out a hand, bracing himself against the seat in front of him. It was a wise move. The whole train shuddered and jerked as the carriages and wagons braked erratically in turn, banging against one another. When the worst of the noise and jolting was over, Lawson relaxed and tried to peer past his companion to the window.

'There must be something on the line,' he said, his voice still carrying the soft burr of the Scottish Highlands he'd left at the age of six. 'Can ye see anything, Sam?' Sam Liston already had his head to the glass, looking towards the front of the train.

'Trees grow pretty close to the tracks up ahead and the road curves round them,' Sam answered. 'I cain't see anything for certain-sure.' His voice was a Kentucky drawl.

Other passengers in the half-full car were looking out too. The view from the windows was spectacular;

a Colorado valley in the foothills of the Rockies, fresh with early summer green. The narrow-gauge train had been heading downgrade from one of the many little mining towns scattered along this stretch of the east side of the Rocky Mountains. They were a little less than an hour's ride from Lucasville, the county seat.

'It could be a landslip,' Sam Liston suggested, slumping back into his seat. 'They call steam trains 'iron horses', but I reckon they're more like mules, myself. Trains and mules both like to stop dead for no reason anyone can tell, and there's sure a lot of cussing afore they move again.'

'I'm sure the engineer knows why we've stopped,' Alec Lawson answered. He leaned into the aisle and looked up and down. 'I hope it is just a wee landslip.'

Sam watched him thoughtfully. 'You've sure got a suspicious mind,' he remarked, guessing what his companion was thinking.

Alec turned and grinned at him. 'Aye, and it's kept us alive often enough.' He leaned forward, on the point of standing up, when the door at the front of the car opened and two men came in.

Both had plain bandannas drawn up over their faces, and each carried a revolver in his right hand.

'Keep still and keep quiet,' the taller bandit ordered, aiming his gun at the nearest man. 'Hand over your money and watches nice an' easy, and no one gets themselves hurt.'

The second bandit held a small burlap sack out to the closest passenger, gesturing with his revolver. The tall one kept his attention on the rest of the passengers.

'Professional,' muttered Sam. In spite of the situation, there was a bright spark of mischief in his eyes.

'So're we,' Alec returned softly. 'Can ye get an angle at them?'

'If they ain't looking.'

Alec Lawson nodded once, his attention on the bandits. He and Sam Liston were five rows along from the front of the car where the bandits had entered. There were just five other passengers between his position and the bandits, and another dozen or so further back. Moving steadily and carefully, Alec slid out of his seat and stood up. The tall bandit quickly saw him and pointed his revolver straight at Alec's head. Alec stopped moving even before the bandit could speak, and held his hands up in plain view.

'Take it easy,' he said, as calmly as he could. 'I'm not dumb enough to try making trouble.'

The tall bandit studied him; his face was mostly hidden by the black bandanna, but his eyes were scornful enough.

Outwardly, Alec Lawson didn't look capable of causing any trouble for a professional pair of outlaws. He stood just below average height and was slender, with small hands. Although in his early thirties, there was a boyishness to his face that made him seem several years younger. His clothes were unremarkable: brown jacket, a collarless cream shirt with a dark-green bandanna tied loosely around his neck, and rust-coloured corduroy trousers tucked into brown riding boots. The gun-belt, with a short-barrelled Artillery Colt on his right and a hunting knife on the left, almost seemed out of place.

Alec carefully kept his hands well clear of his weapons as he moved a step closer to the bandits. The revolver tracked his move, just a few feet away from his face. He fought to keep his hands from twitching with the urge to reach for his gun. 'If I give ye every buck I've got, how about you leave the rest of these folk alone?' he suggested.

Crinkles appeared around the bandit's eyes, suggesting that he was smiling under the bandanna mask. 'Why don't we just take all your dollars and those of everyone else here as well?' he said scornfully. 'You don't look like you've got enough cash to buy us off.'

'I have; I was going to put it in the bank at Lucasville,' Alec said. He slowly lowered his hand, reaching for the inside pocket of his jacket. 'I can show you.'

The bandit's gaze dropped, following the movement of Alec's hand. As Alec touched the pocket, a single shot blasted through the railroad car.

The tall bandit's head snapped back, blood spraying out as he toppled backwards against the other outlaw. He dropped so fast he never got a chance to fire. Alec pulled a hold-out gun from his jacket pocket. The second outlaw was turning towards him, off balance but at this range it was hard to miss. Alec fired as Sam got off his second shot. Both hit, tumbling the outlaw against a seat and on to the floor of the car.

Alec ignored the exclamations and wide-eyed stares of the other passengers. He switched the hold-out gun to his left hand and drew the Colt from its holster. Liston followed as he cautiously examined the two dead men.

'Ye got that one smack between the eyes,' Alec remarked, looking at the taller bandit. Alec was a fair hand with a gun, but Sam Liston had a remarkable gift for shooting that he'd never seen equalled. Without his trust in Sam to make an instant kill, Alec would never have gone empty-handed to an armed outlaw like that.

Sam chuckled. 'I thought he was fit to start choking when you offered to buy him off. That was one dandy diversion, boss.'

Alec straightened up, returning the hold-out gun to his pocket. 'These two can't have been working alone. We'd best go see what their friends are up to.'

A middle-aged woman leaned from her seat and laid her hand on his arm.

'You did a swell job just now, but don't risk yourselves trying to be heroes,' she pleaded, looking back and forth between the two of them. 'Wait and report this to the law when we get into Lucasville.'

Alec smiled brightly at her, his brown eyes suddenly warm and younger. 'We are the law, ma'am.' He pulled back the left side of his jacket to reveal a shield-shaped badge pinned to his shirt. 'Alec Lawson, sheriff of Dereham County, and that's Deputy Sheriff Sam Liston.'

'Alec's also a deputy US marshal, and a captain of the

US Army, retired,' Sam added helpfully.

'I wish you were a bit more retiring sometimes,' Alec replied. 'Come on, let's go earn our pay.' He led the way to the end of the car.

Sam smiled brilliantly at the woman, bowed to her, and followed. He joined Alec on the little platform at the front of the car. At a signal from the sheriff, both men cautiously leaned out and scanned the track on either side of the train.

'Still cain't see anything up ahead,' Sam reported. 'One mounted man standing guard four cars down, about level with a goods wagon.'

'Three mounted men and some packhorses on the other side of the wagon,' Alec said. 'My guess is they're unloading bullion from the mine. Robbing passengers is just a sideline.'

'How do we get close enough to get the jump on them?' Sam asked.

Alec studied the car in front of theirs thoughtfully for a few moments. 'Best chance is to go under,' he said. 'Crawl along the tracks under the train.'

Sam winced but made no other objection.

Alec went first, climbing over the guard rails that surrounded the platform, and squeezing through the narrow gap between cars, down to the track bed. He glanced back up at Sam.

'Ye ken, there are times when it's good to be small.'

Sam grinned back. He was no taller than Alec, but broader in the shoulders and heavier. 'Tell me that again next time you want to reach the coffee when Karl's put it on the top shelf.'

Alec snorted, and knelt down to start working his way under the car. The hardest part was getting under the bogies. He had to lie almost flat, crawling along on elbows and knees. The wheels loomed either side of him, the intricate underparts of the bogie were scant inches above his head. Alec tried very hard not to think about what would happen if the train started moving while he was underneath it. His hat jerked backwards as the low crown brushed against a crossbar. Alec dropped flat, and reached awkwardly to pull his hat back into place.

His main consolation was that at least he was almost impossible to see when under a bogie. Crawling under the main body of the car was easier, and less claustrophobic, but he would be easier to see, especially when he got closer to the outlaws. A few soft curses reassured him that Sam was close behind. More crawling eventually brought them both to the car in front of the wagon that the bandits were emptying. Alec wormed his way under the rear bogie and peered carefully around the rim of the wheel. Sam squeezed up beside him and checked the guard on the other side of the wagon.

'Still in the same place,' he whispered. 'I can only see up as far as the hoss's belly though. It's gonna be plumb tricky to get a shot at him from here.'

Alec had much the same view of the outlaws on his side of the train. He could hear movement in the baggage wagon, and something was passed out to a bandit on foot, who stowed it on a packhorse. The situation wasn't promising for the lawmen, but Alec

11

couldn't stay still and watch a robbery taking place almost under his nose. He could at least count on Sam's full support for whatever he chose to do. They'd met some twelve years ago, as new recruits in the cavalry. They'd started out as bunkies, and the bond established then had stayed firm through two terms of enlistment. They'd ended up as captain and sergeant, a well-established team. Knowing that Sam would follow any plan he came up with was reassuring for Alec, but also a worry. Some day, one of his plans might go wrong and get Sam killed. But, hopefully, it wouldn't be today.

'Best we can do is come out fast and get the drop on them,' Alec said. 'If it comes to shooting, we'll have better cover than them. You keep an eye out for the one on your side; he might come through between these cars and try to get behind us.'

'Ready when you are, boss.' Sam sounded as confident as always.

It took a certain amount of undignified wriggling to get his gun in his hand while lying under the bogie, but Alec managed it. When both men were ready, Alec scrambled forwards. He pushed himself over the rail, rolled, and came neatly up on to his feet, gun aimed at the nearest bandit. A moment later, Sam was beside him, both revolvers covering bandits.

'This is the law!' Alec Lawson barked. 'You're under arrest. Drop your weapons now.' With his left hand, he pulled back his jacket so the badge on his shirt was clearly visible.

The sudden appearance had caught the outlaws by

surprise; none of them had a gun aimed in the right direction. Two of them froze, the other looked to the open door of the baggage wagon. Alec only had a shallow angle of view into the wagon from where he was, but he knew there was another man in there and kept a portion of his attention directed that way. He didn't give the men he could see time to recover from their surprise.

'Your weapons, on the ground, now.' It was a military-sharp order, backed by a commanding glare.

Slowly, one of the mounted outlaws lowered his rifle stock first to the ground. The other began to follow suit, watching the lawmen warily. The man on foot was less visible, half-hidden by the horses. Alec knew that Sam would be watching him, and put more of his attention to the so-far unseen man in the baggage car. A few moments later, a figure appeared abruptly in the open doorway. Even as Alec changed his aim, a voice called.

'Watch where you're aimin', lawman. You don't want to be putting daylight in the mail clerk.'

Alec cursed under his breath. The man visible in the doorway was wearing town clothes, not range clothes, and was unarmed. The look of barely contained fear on his narrow face was evidence enough that the man half-visible behind him was holding a gun to the clerk's head.

'Ye pull that trigger and the charge goes from robbery to murder,' Alec called back.

'You got to catch us first,' the outlaw answered. 'Now you put your guns down, back off along the line but stay

13

where we can see you. Once we're through loading up, we'll be on our way all peaceable-like, and no one gets hurt.'

Alec gritted his teeth, biting down the curses he wanted to spill. He took a deep breath and let it out slowly, fighting to control his frustration. Carefully, not taking his eyes from the outlaws, he bent and placed his Artillery Colt on the ground in front of himself. Liston did the same with his matched Cavalry Colts, and together they backed up half a car's length.

'It's for a fact, you had no choice there,' Sam said quietly.

'I know,' Alec answered, still glaring at the outlaws as they continued shifting bullion from the safe to the packhorses.

His attention was abruptly diverted by noises from behind. He turned to see a cluster of five men, passengers, climbing down from the end of the next car.

'Godammit!' he hissed. With a quick glance back at the outlaws, he turned to face the newcomers. All of them were armed, he saw, and they were ready for trouble. Alec Lawson pulled back his jacket to show his badge.

'Stay where you are,' he ordered. 'Everything's under control.'

'Under control?' repeated the man at the front of the group. He was smartly dressed, but had the look of an outdoor man. He certainly seemed confident with the pocket revolver he carried. With him were two miners, carrying shotguns, and two cowhands, one with a long-barrelled Colt, and one with a rifle. 'If it's under control, why have they still got guns?'

Alec turned his head slightly and spoke over his shoulder. 'Sam?'

'Outlaws are watching them,' Sam Liston reported quietly. 'They getting kinda spooky.'

The group of passengers were still moving forward, guns at the ready. The outlaws wouldn't hesitate to defend themselves, and the two lawmen were standing between the armed groups. Alec started to reach for his hold-out pistol.

'I'm Sheriff Lawson. The bandits have got—'

'Look out!' The cowboy with the rifle snapped off a quick shot.

Alec dropped to the ground, Sam beside him, as gunfire opened up around them. All the passengers fired their weapons, even though the short-range shotguns had no realistic chance of hitting the outlaws. Ignoring them, Alec twisted around to face the bandits. As he looked, the body of the railroad clerk toppled from the doorway of the wagon and landed in an inert heap. The mounted outlaws were returning fire at the passengers, while the man on foot was mounting. Sam was scrabbling his way to where they'd put down their guns.

Alec held his hold-out pistol in both hands and aimed carefully. It was long range for the short-barrelled weapon but he had to try. A fourth bandit jumped from the wagon into the saddle of his horse. More bullets slapped past; the clear mountain air smelt of gunpowder. Someone behind Alec screamed in pain.

Alec fired, and saw the man he'd been aiming at jerk, as though stung by a wasp. The bandits kicked their restless horses into motion. Sam snatched up his Colts and fired from a kneeling position.

A black outlaw swayed in his saddle and dropped his rifle as he fled. Sam paused a moment, assessing the fleeing mob of men and horses, then fired. One of the pack horses stumbled, almost pulling down the riding horse its lead rein was attached to. The packhorse managed to stay on its feet but awkwardly, further hampered by its load. The leader of the outlaws shouted something, and the balding man leading the horse released its lead rope. Another shot from Sam grazed the leader's mount, making it squeal and buck. It didn't slow down, though. A few moments more and the outlaws were beyond effective range of the handguns. The injured packhorse limped a few strides after its companions, then slowed to a halt. The cowhand with the rifle sent some lead after the outlaws, but hit nothing.

When the shooting stopped, Alec got to his feet and walked along to the baggage wagon, pausing to pick up his Colt on the way. He stopped by the crumpled body of the clerk. There was a small hole in the back of the man's head, and a larger, messier one, where the bullet had exited through his forehead. The clerk's eyes were open, as blue as the sky above, and empty of life. Alec looked up from the body as the passengers approached, talking amongst themselves, bragging to one another of how they drove the bandits away. Sam shook his head as he saw the cold fury in Alec Lawson's

16

eyes: when Alec had finished with them, those passengers were going to wish they'd stayed well away from the bandits.

CHAPTER TWO

Alec Lawson made himself take a deep breath and let it out again slowly. He looked at the two men sitting on the far side of his desk, then spoke.

'Mister Anderson, I'm well aware that ten thousand dollars is a lot of money, and I promise ye we'll do all we can to catch the bandits.'

Looking at the well-dressed owner of the Cornucopia Silver Mining Company, the sheriff couldn't help but feel that a sum like ten thousand dollars meant a lot more to himself than it did to K J Anderson. To him, it seemed a vast sum, but that was not the only reason he wanted to catch the bandits who had robbed the train.

'I intend to see the leader brought to justice for the murder of the railroad clerk,' Alec added, looking at his other visitor.

Webb puffed heavily on his short pipe, sending blue smoke into the air of the sheriff's private office. The chairman of the Northern Colorado Railroad was a sturdy, thick-necked man with grey in his reddish hair and a flourishing set of side whiskers. Although his clothes were as good as the mine owner's, Webb looked uncomfortable in them, like a labourer dressed up for a wedding.

'Have you been out looking for them, sheriff?' Webb asked, his voice a rough growl.

'Two of my deputies, Liston and Oldfield, are out searching for them now,' Alec answered. 'They went out yesterday, less than an hour after Liston and I got back here after the robbery.'

'You chose not to go after the bandits yourself,' Anderson remarked, frowning. The mine owner was a long-faced man, whose fine moustache didn't quite hide his large and rather prominent teeth. His light-brown hair was carefully combed and held in place with scented pomade to disguise the fact that it was receding. The long face, large teeth and his general broad, clumsy build put Alec somewhat in mind of a draft horse.

'I have duties that need my attention here,' Alec told the two men. 'Such as talking to ye both about this robbery myself, rather than sending a deputy, and ensuring the safe return of the silver that we managed to prevent the bandits from taking.'

'Hmmm, yes.' Anderson revealed his large teeth in a smile that didn't reach his eyes. 'I'm most grateful to you, Sheriff Lawson, for preventing them from taking more of the silver, most grateful. It is still a heavy blow for the Cornucopia to bear, however.' He turned his attention to Webb. 'We shall be seeking recompense from the Northern Colorado Railroad.'

Webb scowled in return, looking more like a bulldog

19

than ever. 'You won't get it.'

'You failed in your duty to protect the goods entrusted to your care.'

'A man died for the sake of your silver!' Webb protest.

'Perhaps if there had been armed guards in the wagon—' Anderson said.

'You want armed guards, you pay for armed guards.'

'Gentlemen!' Alec waited until both men were looking at him. 'If you want to have an argument, please do so somewhere other than my office. Now, I've shared with you all the information I have on this matter at the moment. Is there anything constructive ye have to offer?'

Webb looked rather surly, but shook his head. Anderson aimed another smile at the sheriff.

'The Cornucopia Silver Mine will offer a reward of one hundred dollars for information leading to the arrest and conviction of any of the persons responsible for the theft of our silver: the arrest and conviction,' he repeated with satisfaction.

'I'll see that's added to the wanted posters,' Alec promised. 'Now, if there's nothing more I can do for you gentlemen, I'm sure you're busy men.' He rose, encouraging them to rise as well.

Anderson leaned over the desk to enfold Alec's hand in his own broad one, and shake it vigorously. 'Glad to be dealing with you, Sheriff Lawson. I'm sure we understand one another.'

Alec simply nodded and smiled, withdrawing his hand as soon as decently possible. To his relief, Webb didn't offer to shake hands, but nodded at him, and ejected another puff of smoke from his pipe. Webb left without looking back, while Anderson paused for another ingratiating smile and a half-bow before leaving Alec alone.

Alec made a brief note about the reward on the edge of his blotting paper, then put the pencil down and sat still for a few moments to relish the quiet. Not that the room was completely silent. The building where he and his deputies lived and worked was on one of the main roads of Lucasville. The sound of hoofs, of creaking and rumbling wheels, shouts, laughter and faint music from someone playing a harmonica, all came through the propped-open window. They were the usual sounds of town life, though, and didn't disturb him in the least. Alec picked up the new copy of the *Lucasville Trumpet*, the town's weekly newspaper, and attempted to waft pipe smoke towards the window. The smell lingered, though, like the bad temper the two businessmen induced in him.

Dropping the newspaper back on to his otherwise tidy desk, Alec rose and stretched. He picked up his brown gun-belt from its peg and buckled it on, then collected his hat and made his way through to the larger office. The two offices occupied the front half of the sheriff's building. The front door of the building led into the large office, where his three deputies worked. The desks, chairs and filing cabinets were plain and functional, but the room had nonetheless acquired some character from the men who occupied it.

Behind Sam Liston's desk, three colourized pictures

21

of showgirls were pinned to the wall, with the withered remains of a red rose tucked into the top of one image. The desk was the untidiest in the room, littered with odds and ends of papers, two brass buttons and a tin mug with half an inch of cold coffee in the bottom. Ethan Oldfield's desk sported a calendar with sentimental pictures of young women and a jar of patent hair cream. Karl Firth's desk was as neatly organized as Lawson's own. On the wall behind it was a framed photograph of the four men, all smartly turned out in dress uniform, taken just before Alec and Sam had finished their second terms of enlistment.

Karl Firth looked up from his writing as Alec left his office. His fair, aristocratic good looks betrayed his German ancestry more than his family name, which had been changed three generations back. He was the tallest, and marginally the oldest, of the four lawmen. Unlike the other three, Karl had attended a military academy and had joined the company as a lieutenant, alongside Alec. The difference in their backgrounds had jarred at first, but the necessity of working together had forged trust and friendship that had lasted.

Karl studied Alec's face. 'They wanted to know why you haven't already tracked down and arrested every single outlaw who took part in the train robbery?' he guessed.

Alec snorted. 'Ten thousand dollars in silver stolen, and a harmless clerk murdered, and K J Anderson offers a reward of one hundred dollars. He's a close chewer and a tight spitter; that's nothing but loose change to him. Ye'd think he didn't want anyone bothering to go after the outlaws.'

'He'd most likely say that a man doesn't get rich by spending money he doesn't need to,' Karl answered. 'Going to be out for long?'

Alec shook his head. 'I want a breath of fresh air, mebbe get some coffee. I'll see you soon.'

Karl nodded and lifted a hand in a farewell gesture as Alec left the office.

Alec strolled along the sidewalk, watching the everyday bustle of the thriving small town, built in the eastern foothills of the Rockies. Away to the east swept the high plains – an endless sea of fertile grassland that was rapidly being turned into good agricultural land. A few miles to the west of Lucasville rose the first peaks of the Rocky Mountains, forested in lush trees and bearing gold and silver in the rocks beneath the surface. The little town thrived on both the mining and the agriculture, and served as county seat for Dereham County, Alec's jurisdiction as sheriff.

A wagon laden with sawn lumber rumbled past, driven by a fresh-faced young man of about seventeen. He reminded Alec of himself at a similar age, in a job he'd had delivering for a butcher. It had been an undemanding job, at a time when his only responsibility had been to himself. His chief concern had been getting the right package to the right customer. If anything had gone wrong, it had been a nuisance, but not a disaster. Now, though, a mistake in his work could mean a death on his conscience, like the railroad clerk.

Leaving the busy street, Alec wandered through a quieter section of town. The air was fresher here than in his office, though nothing like as crisp as it was up in the Rockies. The town smelt of burning wood and coal, of horses and manure and of a general staleness compounded of sweat and decaying rubbish. All the same, it was good to be outdoors. Alec relished the feel of the breeze on his face, and the warmth of the late May sunshine. He began to relax, his worries over robberies and squabbling businessmen becoming less urgent as he strolled along.

Even with his attention elsewhere, Alec's lawman instincts were still alert. Keeping law and order within Lucasville itself was the job of the town's marshal and his officers, but Alec's sense of duty meant getting involved anywhere he saw trouble. He knew that the three men clustered further along the narrow street were trouble, even before he saw the woman. Alec's attention snapped sharply into the present as he studied the situation. Three heavy-set men, most likely miners, had surrounded a woman. The group were some thirty feet away from Alec, the woman with her back against the lumber wall of a house, while the men stood around her. From what Alec could see of her, she was respectably dressed, her hair hidden by a stylish cream hat.

'You got time to stop an' talk,' one of the men was saying to her.

'We sure ain't in no hurry,' added one with a crooked nose. He leaned rather close and smiled at her. 'Come an' have a drink with us.'

24

'We'd sure admire to have your company,' the third one put in.

'No, thank you,' she said firmly. 'I have shopping to do.'

'Why, the stores won't close for hours yet,' Crooked Nose said. 'What you got to get back for?'

Alec unfastened his jacket with his left hand, pushing it back to show the badge pinned to his shirt, and checked the set of his revolver with his other hand. He stepped forward briskly and spoke up.

'The lady said she's not interested.'

The miners turned to look at him. All three were taller and stronger than Alec, and Crooked Nose started to smile. It was an expression Alec had seen many times before from men bigger than himself. He spoke quickly, before any of the miners could issue a challenge.

'I'm Sheriff Lawson.' He indicated the shield-shaped badge. 'Sheriff of this county. This badge gives me the right to tell ye to move on, or to arrest ye. And this Colt gives me the ability to enforce what I tell ye.' He stopped a few feet away from the nearest man and looked at each in turn. 'If ye want a woman's company, go to a saloon or one of the houses with a red lamp in the window. If I see any of ye bothering a decent woman again, you'll be behind bars so fast your head'll spin.'

Two of the men sidled away from the woman, leaving Crooked Nose to face the sheriff. Crooked Nose continued to stare, but he wasn't smiling any more.

'What's your name?' Alec snapped.

Crooked Nose scowled, then glanced at the woman

and drew himself upright. 'Tom Dench,' he answered defiantly, looking to see that she'd registered his name.

'Where do you work?' Alec asked.

When Dench didn't answer, one of his friends spoke up. 'We work at the Liberty Bell.'

Alec recognized it as the name of a mine near the mouth of Red Hill Gulch.

Dench continued to stare insolently at the sheriff, showing no signs of moving.

'You'd shoot an unarmed man?' he drawled.

'I'd shoot an unarmed man who was pestering a decent woman,' Alec replied unflinchingly. 'I don't have to shoot to kill, but if I did, most folks would figure ye'd deserved it.'

Dench dropped his gaze briefly, and Alec knew he was winning the battle of wills. He flicked a glance at one of the other men. The miner cleared his throat before speaking up.

'I got me a powerful thirst, Tom. Let's go settle the dust with some beer.'

Alec stepped to one side, giving them plenty of room to walk past. The one that had spoken began to move. Dench reluctantly went with him, the third one tagging behind. Alec watched them steadily as they passed, keeping most of his attention on Tom Dench. The miner's expression was surly, but Alec could tell he wasn't drunk enough to start a fight with a lawman. Dench paused after passing Alec, looking back at the woman. He gave Alec a thoughtful look, then slouched after his friends. Only when the miners had reached the end of the narrow street did Alec relax and turn to the woman.

He saw at once that she was almost as tall as he was, graceful and slender. She was beautiful, but the intelligence in her brown eyes and her calm confidence were what inspired him to smile at her.

'Are ye all right, ma'am?' he asked, raising his hat politely.

She smiled back. 'I'm just fine, thank you. I do appreciate your intervention, Sheriff.'

'Sheriff Lawson, Alec Lawson. I haven't seen ye in town before?'

'I arrived four days ago,' she explained. 'I'm Mrs Wessex; Eileen Wessex.' Alec felt a pang of disappointment at learning she was married, but kept his feelings from his face. 'What does your husband do?' he asked politely.

Something in her eyes changed. 'He passed away last year. I decided to come out West and teach school.'

'Oh, I'm sorry.' Annoyance at himself for his tactlessness jarred with the pleasure at knowing she no longer had a husband. 'I hope—' he stopped, not sure what he was hoping for.

She smiled softly at him. 'I wanted to get away from old memories and find myself a new and maybe useful way of occupying myself. I taught school for a couple of years before I was married and I found it rewarding.'

'Well, I hope you'll be happy in Lucasville, Mrs Wessex.' Alec softened the rather awkward words with another smile.

'Thank you,' she answered. 'I'm pleased to have met you, Sheriff Lawson. I'd best let you get on your way.'

'I guess so.' Alec hadn't been going anywhere in particular but he didn't want to make a nuisance of himself. He nodded politely to Eileen Wessex and walked away rather briskly. The problems of railroad robberies and businessmen were temporarily forgotten.

CHAPTER THREE

'Boss, this is a wild goose chase. Can't we just go home?'

Alec Lawson reined in his blowing horse and looked across at his companion, Ethan Oldfield. The deputy sheriff was taller and rangier than Alec, with a long face that tended towards mournful expressions. He wore unremarkable range clothes in brown and blue with only the Sioux beadwork on his knife's sheath as decoration.

'If you and Sam hadn't lost the train robbers' trail, we could be sure we were looking in the right place,' Alec answered. 'Anyway, even if we don't find them in Caribou, it's been a wonderful ride. Just look at that view.' He gestured at the spectacular mountain scenery around them.

Ethan looked pained. 'Alec, we live in Colorado. The only thing this state's got more of than mines is scenery.'

Alec chuckled. Ethan Oldfield's dour outlook was like Sam Liston's vanity; both were real character traits that were deliberately exaggerated.

'Then I'm glad I like a wee bit of scenery,' Alec

remarked. He nudged his horse into a walk again. Ethan's sigh was perfectly audible, but he followed along the mountain trail without verbal complaint.

While Ethan and Sam had been on their futile attempt to track the robbers from the scene of the train robbery, Alec had been spending time looking through all the wanted dodgers available in the office. Neither he nor Sam had got a good look at the man who'd shot the railroad clerk, but Alec had eventually put a name to one of the other faces at the baggage car, a man named Shotton. He'd also identified the bandit that Sam had plugged between the eyes. Both men had been known to frequent the saloon in the mining town of Caribou, so Alec had decided to head out that way in search of more information.

The little town was a tough, thirty-mile ride from Lucasville, climbing steadily up into the Rockies. Alec and Ethan had broken the journey overnight at Jamestown, setting off again in the cool, spring morning. As Alec had said, the scenery here was spectacular, and the stagecoach trail they were following would soon be carrying summer sightseers as well as miners, hauliers and other folk connected with the mining industry.

They reached the crest of the trail, and another valley came into view, sheltering between the steep walls of the mountains. Sections of the sharp-scented pine woods had been cleared away where the mines and the town flourished. From this high point of the trail, Lawson could count four large mines, the buildings clinging to the sides of the valley, and he knew of two more in the immediate area. Dark smoke rising into the brilliantly blue sky told them where the town was, even though the buildings were largely hidden by patches of forest.

Alec pulled up to let his dun gelding take a brief rest. He sat relaxed in his deep saddle and gazed contentedly at the view, comparing it to his early childhood memories of the Scottish Highlands. Scotland was nothing like so spectacular as this, but he sometimes felt that those now distant roots were why he loved this magnificent country so. Ethan was rather more prosaic.

'Iffen we push on, we can get dinner in Caribou and get back to Jamestown by night,' he suggested.

Alec sighed, and nudged his horse into a walk.

Half an hour later, they'd reached Caribou. The buildings at the centre of town were well made and substantial: two banks, a hotel, stores, a restaurant, three saloons and a livery stable. As the town straggled away from the main street, the buildings became rougher, with less planning. On the west of town, the land sloped steeply upwards, so some buildings had doors level with the roofs of their downslope neighbours. There was activity on the streets, mostly of goods being loaded and unloaded, but any noise made by the hauliers and their mules was largely drowned out by the constant pounding of the mills and the sound of the lumber mill at the far end of town.

As the lawmen rode past the outlying buildings, Lawson's attention was drawn to a scruffy saloon. Its walls were of roughly sawn lumber, and the roof was

31

comprised of tarpaulin. A crudely painted sign nailed above the door named it as the 'Silver Doller'.

'You'd reckon that someone who runs a business would know how to spell "dollar",' Ethan remarked.

'I don't recall seeing that place last time I was out this way,' Alec said.

'Boards aren't weathered yet,' Ethan pointed out. 'It can't have been here long.'

'I bet the owner hasn't even applied for a licence yet,' Alec said. As county sheriff, issuing licences for all kinds of businesses was part of his job. 'Better go have a word with them.'

They hitched their horses to a rail that looked hardly strong enough to restrain a week-old foal, and entered the dimly lit saloon. Pausing just inside, to let his eyes adjust to the low light, Alec Lawson looked around. The floor was hard-packed dirt and most of the furniture looked as though it had been cobbled together from offcuts left from building the walls. The only decorations were a few paper pictures of fashionably dressed women, glued to the walls. Alec couldn't be sure, but he suspected the pictures were pages from a copy of 'Godey's Lady's Magazine'. The air was stuffy, and smelt of stale beer, stale bodies and stale smoke.

'What a charming place,' murmured Ethan, as they made their way to the bar. 'I'm not surprised it's so busy.'

Although the room could probably hold a hundred people, there were no more than a dozen present aside from themselves. At one table, a bored faro dealer was turning the cards for two equally bored players. A lone

Chinaman was savouring his glass of beer. One large table was occupied by half a dozen men eating dinner, while two others sat in the most distant corner, sipping whiskey. The barman looked up from the crumpled newspaper he was reading as the lawmen reached the bar.

'If you want food, eggs are off, but the cook's a mean hand with pork belly,' he said.

Alec shook his head. 'No thanks. I just want to see your liquor licence.'

The barman blinked. 'Liquor licence? What business is—?'

His words cut off short as Alec pushed his jacket back to reveal the badge pinned to his shirt.

'Alec Lawson, Dereham County Sheriff. Which makes your lack of a liquor licence my business.'

The barman's bushy brows drew together in a frown. 'Haven't you got any real work to do? Like catching horse-thieves or claim jumpers?'

Alec had heard this complaint dozens of times before. He just stared straight back at the bartender. 'County law says that any premises which sells intoxicating liquor has got to have a licence. Some folks just aren't fit to be selling liquor; we got to have a way so we can stop them doing it.'

The barman snorted, as if unconvinced, but he dropped his gaze from Alec's.

'I'll have to close up, or else hire staff to cover while I ride into Lucasville to get the damn licence,' he grumbled.

'If you apply for the licence within ten days of now,

I'll not bother about the weeks you've been operating without one,' Alec promised.

The bartender winced at that, then nodded. 'I'll be there.'

'See that you—' Alec's warning was cut off by an urgent warning from Ethan.

'Boss!'

Alec heard the rasp of Ethan's Army Colt leaving its holster, and whipped around to see what was happening.

A gunshot crashed out, and a beer glass a little further along the bar erupted into shards. Alec knew at once that the shot had come from where the group of men had been eating. As he continued his turn to face their way, he was also moving away from the bar and drawing his own gun. Two of the men from the table were making for a door at the rear of the saloon, the others were firing. More bullets tore into the bar and the wall behind it. Alec heard the crack of a bullet missing his head by inches. He dived for the cover of the nearest table even as he realized that he'd seen one of the gunmen before.

Ethan was moving too, firing once before joining Alec in the poor cover of the shabby table. A bullet ripped into the dirt floor next to Ethan's left foot. He pulled his foot in hastily, trying to make himself as small a target as possible.

'Table over,' Alec ordered, grabbing the nearest table leg.

Ethan seized hold of another, and between them they swiftly upended the table, improving their shelter.

A slug smacked into the tabletop just in front of Alec's face. The wood cracked but the bullet didn't get through. His heart jumped at the close call but he didn't panic.

'I guess these folks don't agree with licences for saloons either,' Ethan said. Alec fired a couple of blind shots from behind the table, sighting by instinct, then popped his head out for a quick look. A return shot slapped past as he retreated back behind the table.

'Thought so,' he said, dumped used shells from his Colt. 'That balding one in the dark blue shirt is Shotton, part of the gang that held up the train. I'm not sure about the others, but him I definitely recognize.'

Ethan snorted as he also reloaded. 'So you guessed right about them being based in Caribou. They've also got us pinned down and they outnumber us. How's your canny Scottish mind going to get us out of this mess?'

Alec risked another quick look through the haze of gunpowder that was filling the room.

'You're coming at this all wrong,' he replied. 'We've got them on the run.' Two more bullets ploughed into the table top, which was beginning to splinter ominously. Ethan flinched as wooden splinters sprayed close to his face.

'I think one of them's wounded; the black one that Sam shot,' Alec went on. Ethan fired another couple of rounds over the table as Alec talked.

'You head left while I cover,' Alec ordered. 'Get spread out before they send someone round behind us.' He pulled his hold-out gun from his inner pocket.

Ethan nodded, and took a look at the empty table that would be his next cover. He quickly gauged distances, and said, 'Ready.'

Alec Lawson sprang up suddenly, both guns blazing. He was aware of Ethan lunging away in a flurry of movement, but couldn't spare a moment to watch. Through the gunsmoke, he saw the bandits who'd been firing at them duck suddenly. His unexpected assault had panicked them momentarily, buying Ethan the time he needed to get into fresh cover. The other patrons of the saloon were out of sight, hiding under their tables. As his guns crashed, and his heart raced, Alec caught brief impressions of the men he was fighting. One had red hair, another was fair. Another had black hair and wore mostly dark clothing. A fourth seemed older than the others, with grey touching his brown hair. Then the bandits began to return fire.

Ethan threw himself under a table, cursing breathlessly as he banged into the legs. The table rocked with the impact, and he used the momentum to tip it over, getting the top between himself and the bandits. Alec half saw all this as a blur from the corner of his eye. His main concern was with the bandits. Two had reached the rear door and were on their way out. One of them was a black man, like the one Sam had wounded during the train robbery. He was moving awkwardly, but Alec couldn't spare the time for a good look at him. The man in dark clothes shouted encouragement to his companions as they fired. Lead ploughed into the table in front of Alec, and more zipped past him, close enough to tear his sleeve.

Alec ducked back, gasping for breath. He dropped the hold-out gun and began reloading his Colt even as more rounds slammed into the increasingly battered table that sheltered him. As Alec stopped firing, Ethan rose and directed fire at the bandits. Hidden behind his table, Alec heard a rapid exchange of shots. He glanced up in time to see Ethan's brown hat jerk off backwards, and Ethan drop back into shelter. For a moment, Alec feared the worst, but he soon saw that Ethan was unhurt.

The two lawmen looked at one another. The shooting had died down. Alec could hear sounds of movement from the bandits' direction, and guessed that they were trying to make a break for the back door. He held his gun up, to signal readiness to Ethan. The deputy slipped a couple of fresh shells into his long-barrelled Colt, and did the same. Alec held up three fingers, mouthing the countdown as he folded down each finger in turn. When he reached zero, the two lawmen popped up simultaneously, and began firing.

Alec had guessed right; the bandits were trying to run. He fired a couple of shots at the nearest target and was rewarded by seeing the fair-haired outlaw stumble and fall to his knees, crying out in pain. As the other bandits kept going, ducking and weaving, the injured man yelled after them.

'Help me, Don—'

The man in dark clothes turned, bringing his gun around in one smooth move. He fired, cutting off the plea for help with a single shot. The fair-haired man jerked, blood spraying against the wall, and fell limply.

37

His killer fired again, spraying fast shots in Alec's direction as he backed towards the door. Alec ducked behind the table as he saw the gun aimed his way. Bullets slapped just over his head, and another ripped through the battered table, spraying more splinters against his face. Alec pushed his gun round the edge of the table and let off a couple of blind shots.

A few moments later, all was quiet. Alec lifted his head cautiously, feeling warm blood sliding down his cheek, and looked across at Ethan. The deputy was hunkered down behind his own table, his long face as mournful as ever as he returned the sheriff's look. He shrugged, then slowly peered around the edge of his table. There was no response.

'They've gone, boss,' Ethan said.

Alec let out a long breath, feeling some of the tension start to ebb. He found a few fresh bullets on his gunbelt, and slipped them into his gun. That done, he dabbed a handkerchief against his face, mopping up most of the blood. He rose and cautiously made his way across to the body the bandits had left behind. Chairs and furniture scraped as the saloon's other patrons came out from their hiding places. Alec didn't need to examine the body closely to see if the fair-haired man was dead: the mess where a bullet had torn through his head from close range was clear enough.

As Ethan joined him, Alec knelt down and quickly searched the man's pockets.

'Did you hear what he called the feller in black?' Ethan asked.

'Sound like Don, or Donny,' Alec answered,

removing a pocketbook and briefly inspecting the contents.

'Don sure seems kind of touchy about having folks shout it out in public,' Ethan remarked.

Alec stuffed the pocketbook into his own jacket pocket, to prevent any opportunist from stealing it, and stood up. 'Come on. If we get mounted up, we might be able to catch up with them.' He turned and headed briskly back across the saloon. As he passed the bar, he called out to the barkeep. 'Don't touch that body. We'll be back soon enough, and I want to find everything there as I left it.'

The barkeep nodded sullenly as Alec and Ethan made their way back outside.

Alec took a deep breath of the clean mountain air, appreciating its freshness after the stink of beer and gunpowder in the saloon. His horse whickered softly as he approached, turning its ears in his direction.

'Good fellow, Biscuit,' Alec said, patting the pale dun horse on its creamy-yellow neck as he unhitched the reins with his other hand.

Vaulting easily into the deep saddle, Alec turned his horse up the street. With Ethan beside him, Alec jogged his horse around the side of the shanty saloon. When he reached the back, there was no sign of the bandits, just a solitary bay horse in the small corral, gazing at an alleyway between the rough buildings that sprawled back of the saloon. Alec guessed that the bay was looking where its companions had gone, and urged his dun in that direction. He rode past the corral and turned between two log-framed shacks. He was just in time to glimpse a couple of horses as they disappeared around the far side of a shack further along the row. The bay in the corral whinnied forlornly as the lawmen rode past.

Alec pushed his horse into a canter, drawing his gun as he headed after the fleeing outlaws. They were heading uphill, into the dense stands of aromatic pine and spruce that flooded the steep sides of the valley. The sheriff had no need to look at Ethan, and check what he was doing. He knew that Ethan would have drawn his gun too, and would be ready for action. Alec half-rose in his stirrups as he approached the corner, thumbing back the hammer of his Colt. The precaution was unnecessary; as he rounded the corner, all he saw was an empty path between buildings, leading into the forest of pine and spruce.

The dun was glad to come to a halt on the steep uphill slope. Alec peered into the dark green mass of trees, absently noting the way the limber pine grew at crazy angles on the rocks that jutted from the valley side.

'We're not following, boss?' Ethan asked, reining his mount in beside Alec's.

The sheriff shook his head. 'Too many places among the trees where they could hole up and get the drop on us as we chased them.'

Ethan's long face grew suspicious as he peered into the trees. 'Could be one in there now, settling his sights on us,' he said mournfully.

'Aye, there might well be,' Alec agreed, smiling suddenly. 'We'd best be getting back to the Silver Dollar to pick up the one they left behind.'

He turned his horse and rode back, holstering his gun.

'That one, Don, was pretty ruthless about killing his own man, rather than risking him telling us anything,' Oldfield commented, as he followed. 'I reckon he could be some ruthless towards anyone trying to catch him.'

That thought had occurred to Lawson, which was the main reason he'd not followed the bandits into the thick cover of the trees. It wasn't a reassuring thought.

CHAPTER FOUR

'You've identified the outlaws who stole my bullion from the train?' K J Anderson asked, watching the sheriff intently as he waited for the response.

Sheriff Lawson nodded. 'Aye, I believe so. The one killed up in Caribou is definitely Bobby Rockline; he had a history of robbery, rustling and the like. I'm pretty sure that the man who killed him is Al Donegan.' The sheriff shuffled through a handful of wanted notices he had on his desk, and handed one over to Anderson.

The mine owner looked at it, without bothering to read it in detail; he knew plenty about Donegan already.

'He seems like a real tail-twister,' Anderson said. 'A tail-twister.'

The sheriff snorted. 'He killed one of his men, rather than risk him spilling any information to us. Rockline is no loss to society, but I reckon it was Donegan who murdered the mail clerk on the train.'

'You may be right,' Anderson said, nodding wisely.

He handed the paper back across the desk, studying the sheriff as he did so. Lawson had been much quicker at identifying the railroad bandits than Anderson had expected, and had come mighty close to getting his hands on Donegan. Anderson had heard nothing but good reports of Sheriff Lawson and his deputies, but he'd never had much contact with the man before now. Anderson realized that at their first meeting, he'd let himself be deceived by the sheriff's small stature and apparently mild demeanour. Looking again now, he could see the strength of character in Lawson's eyes.

'Do you know where Donegan might be now?' Anderson asked.

The sheriff grimaced slightly. 'Unfortunately, no. If he's any sense, he's moved out of Dereham County altogether. I've wired other county sheriffs to watch out for him.'

Anderson nodded; that was the efficient sort of reaction he was coming to expect from this man. The mine owner produced a smile, showing off his rather large and prominent teeth.

'What would you do if he showed up in Dereham County again?' he asked.

'Go after him and nail his hide for the murder of the railroad clerk and the robbery,' Lawson replied rather sharply.

'Of course, of course,' Anderson murmured.

'I'm a Deputy US Marshal, as well as sheriff of this county,' Lawson went on. 'So I've got jurisdiction to chase felons anywhere in Colorado.'

Anderson had forgotten Lawson's dual status; he covered his surprise with another smile, as he revised his estimate of the sheriff's income.

K J Anderson's love was money. Not merely for itself, but for the security it represented. The more money that accumulated in his bank accounts, the safer he felt from the whims of man and fate. Every cent he possessed had to earn its keep. His clothes were good enough for a man of his position in town, but no more expensive than necessary. Likewise his house, furnishings and horses. He could estimate to within a few cents the value of the clothes that Lawson wore, and of the few personal belongings in the sheriff's office. The sheriff's clothes were of decent quality, but by no means new. The sleeve suspenders on his shirt suggested that his cream cotton shirt was off-the-shelf, not tailor-made for a man of his height.

To Anderson, it was clear that Sheriff Lawson didn't like to waste the money he was getting from his two jobs. No doubt he preferred to bank it, just as the mine owner did himself. That made money a weakness for the sheriff, a possible way of keeping some control over him. Anderson smiled at the thought, more genuinely than before. He didn't like the idea of spending money on bribes, but if it kept this sheriff from making a nuisance of himself in Anderson's affairs, it would be a worthwhile investment.

'Donegan could sure be in for a surprise then, if he thinks he can lose you just by slipping over a county border,' Anderson remarked.

'That's so,' Lawson agreed. He leaned back in his chair, tapping his fingers lightly on his desk. 'Was there anything else you wanted?'

Anderson considered; he now knew how much the

sheriff knew about the train robbers, and some more about the sheriff himself. He wanted to learn more about Lawson, but not by asking directly. With that thought, he shook his head.

'I sure appreciate you letting me take up your time like this,' he said, leaning over to shake hands. 'I surely appreciate it. You understand I'm keen to know if there's any chance of getting that silver back. And seeing whoever killed the railroad clerk behind bars,' he added.

Standing, he carefully adjusted his hat over his receding hair. 'Thank you for your time, Sheriff,' he repeated.

With a polite nod of the head, K J Anderson left the sheriff's office.

A short stroll brought him to the office of the town's newspaper, the *Lucasville Trumpet*. The front of the single-storey lumber building was embellished with a large sign depicting the paper's banner, along with smaller signs offering print services for flyers, posters and other jobs. The door led straight into the main print shop, which smelt of metal and ink. One of the typesetters left his table and came to meet Anderson by the front desk.

'O'Connell?' the typesetter asked, inclining his head in the direction of the editor's office.

'Tell him K J Anderson wants to see him,' the mine owner replied.

The typesetter nodded, wiped an inky finger across his chin, and went to deliver the message.

Anderson drummed his fingers on the countertop

45

for the brief time until he was invited into O'Connell's office in the far corner of the building. Once inside the office, he sat down and studied the newspaper editor. O'Connell was a brawny man in his late thirties, with a weathered face decorated by a full, droopy moustache. Although his tools were now pens and a Remington typewriter, his broad hands were still as callused and tough as a labourer's.

O'Connell sucked noisily on his teeth before speaking. 'What can I be doing for you?'

'I've just been talking to Sheriff Lawson,' Anderson said, removing his hat and smoothing down his receding hair. 'He's an interesting man, a most interesting man.'

'A good soldier,' O'Connell said approvingly. 'Cavalry, mind you, not infantry, but I hear tell he enlisted as a private, and finished up as a captain. Most enlisted men don't stand a snowball in hell's chance of getting an officer's commission.'

'Didn't his deputies serve with him?' Anderson asked.

O'Connell nodded, sucking on his teeth again before answering aloud. 'All three of them. I reckon them staying on under his command in civilian life means he was an officer worth his salt, and you don't find too many of those in Uncle Sam's army.'

'But he quit the Army and went into law work instead,' Anderson remarked. 'Does being a good soldier make for being a good sheriff?'

O'Connell shrugged his broad shoulders. 'Lawson ain't done a bad job so far. He ain't afraid to get his hands dirty in a fight, if so he has to, but he don't go round making like some kind of *pistolero*.'

It was clear enough to Anderson that O'Connell respected the lawman and was inclined to defend his reputation.

'You'd vote for Lawson if he runs for sheriff again?' Anderson asked.

He listened as the newspaper editor talked on about the lawman. A few questions thrown into the conversation got him the information he wanted. After five minutes or so, Anderson knew roughly how much Lawson earned, and that, as he'd guessed, the sheriff seemed more inclined to bank his money than spend it. Lawson was known to drink whiskey and gamble, but in moderation. It seemed to confirm what Anderson had already decided: that Lawson's biggest weakness was money.

'Well, I'm for-sure glad there's a good man like Lawson on the trail of the outlaws that stole my bullion,' Anderson said at last, ready to change the subject. 'Though if the Northern Colorado Railroad took more care, that silver wouldn't have been stolen.'

O'Connell looked at the mine owner thoughtfully. 'The railroad takes money to deliver goods, but don't care too hard if the goods make it to where they should go?' he remarked.

'It could be seen in that light,' Anderson agreed, with an ingratiating smile. 'And those bandits that attacked the train also stole from the passengers and put their lives at risk.'

'So transporting bullion alongside of passengers

47

could put the passengers in danger,' said O'Connell. 'I could work that up into something.' He looked at Anderson expectantly.

Anderson fetched out his wallet, took out some paper money and put it on the editor's desk. 'I need to renew my subscription, don't I?' he commented.

O'Connell picked up the cash and counted it swiftly. 'I reckon you owe another ten.'

Anderson stared across at him. 'I expect to get good value for my money.'

'You will.'

Reluctantly, Anderson handed over another ten dollars. He silently reminded himself that he was making an investment, and that he'd earn back all the money he'd paid to the editor, and more, in the long term. This was no different from investing money in machinery for his mine. Pocketing the wallet, he rose, and shook hands with O'Connell.

'I'll see myself out,' Anderson said.

In fact, when he left the newspaper office, he was so occupied with his thoughts, he collided with a woman passing on the sidewalk.

'I beg your pardon,' Anderson said, helping her to pick up the schoolbooks she'd dropped. 'My fault entirely; my fault.'

'No harm was done,' she answered calmly, packing the books back into a basket.

Anderson automatically glanced at her clothes, noting that they were of good quality and respectable, though not as elaborate and stylish as his wife's. Only then did he notice that she was beautiful.

'I do apologize,' Anderson said again, raising his hat to her.

She accepted the apology with a nod, and went on her way again, moving gracefully.

Anderson turned in the other direction, his thoughts returning to Sheriff Lawson.

Alec Lawson opened the cupboard, and glowered up at the tin of coffee beans perched on the top shelf.

'If you're gonna keep putting the coffee up there, ye can make it yoursel',' he growled.

'You make lousy coffee anyway,' Karl Firth told him, reaching up easily to retrieve the tin.

'The only thing you can cook good is porridge,' Sam remarked, from his place at the kitchen table. 'And only a Scot'd want to eat that.'

'You were grateful enough for my porridge when we were bunkies in the barracks,' Alec replied, setting a frying pan on the stove.

'Well, I warn't but a lil' Kentucky boy, fresh off the farm,' Sam drawled. 'I didn't know no better then.'

'If you thought Alec's porridge was good, your mother must have been a lousy cook,' Karl put in, pouring coffee beans into the mill.

Sam put on a wounded expression as Alec chuckled.

The door between the offices at the front of the building, and the living quarters at the back opened as Ethan Oldfield came through. He hid a yawn with the back of his hand as he ambled across to the cookstove.

'Someone had shoved this under the door,' he said, holding a folded piece of paper towards Alec.

Alec dropped a lump of lard into the frying pan and took the paper.

'I told you there was a draft under that door,' Ethan added, peering at the half-inch of cold coffee in the bottom of his tin mug.

'I bet you-all it's a love letter,' Sam said, his eyes sparkling with mischief as he watched the sheriff read the note. 'My money's on a redhead.'

'Ladies don't write notes on paper like that,' Ethan pointed out.

'I never said she was a lady.'

Ethan grunted. 'I don't think it's from a woman. But I bet you it means work for someone,' he said gloomily. 'Most likely getting shot at.'

Alec gazed thoughtfully at the paper before looking up and grinning in a way that worried his comrades.

'The good news, Ethan, is that you're right about this meaning work for someone. The bad news is that it's gonna have to be you three.' He passed the note to Karl. 'Donegan's been sighted in Ballarat; he was there yesterday. I can't go. I've got that tax auction in Jamestown to handle today, but I want you three to head on up to Ballarat and see if you can find him.'

Karl nodded. 'We'll go take a look-see up there.'

'So you get to sit in a saloon and handle the sale of a ranch, while the rest of us go track down some dangerous outlaws, and maybe get ourselves shot at?' Ethan asked, his long face mournful.

Alec nodded cheerfully, dropping slices of bacon into the frying pan.

'It could be a hoax,' Sam pointed out.

'Could be,' Alec agreed. 'In which case, you don't risk getting shot at. But we can't afford to ignore it. You might find Donegan's been and gone already, but you still might pick up his trail. Just be careful if you do run across him,' he added more seriously. 'He's a real mean bastard.'

'I'll remember,' Karl promised.

That afternoon, while Alec Lawson was busy with the tax auction in Jamestown, and his deputies were in Ballarat, another train was robbed ten miles outside Lucasville.

CHAPTER FIVE

A few days later, Alec Lawson lookcd up as the door to his office opened and Sam Liston put his head in the room.

'There's a for-real lady come to see you, boss,' he said, adding a knowing wink. Alec sighed. 'Show her in,' he said, putting his pen on its stand and reaching for the blotting paper. Sam's behaviour was forgotten as soon as the door opened properly and Eileen Wessex entered. Alec stood up hastily and moved around his desk to offer a chair, smiling broadly.

'Mrs Wessex, how nice to see you.' He took her gloved hand. 'Would ye like some coffee?'

She smiled in return. 'That would be lovely, thank you.'

'I'll get it,' Sam volunteered, closing the office door as he left.

Eileen Wessex sat down as Alec returned to his seat behind the desk. He gazed at her, happy to see that she was as lovely as he remembered. Today she wore a stylish outfit in two shades of blue with cream piping, and the same cream straw hat he'd seen before.

'How are ye settling in Lucasville?' Alec asked.

'I like it,' she answered decidedly. 'The air here is wonderful, so clean and sweet. The scenery is magnificent; when I have some more free time, I intend to take the train higher into the mountains and spend some time up there.'

'Georgetown is one of the best places to visit,' Alec told her. 'It's truly beautiful, and from there ye could take the stage to Hot Sulphur Springs, and try the waters.'

'I've never tried a mineral spring,' Eileen admitted. 'I think I shall someday, though. After all, it seems a shame to live so close to some of the finest in the country and not do so.'

Alec nodded, pleased that she liked this country that he admired so much. 'How are ye getting on at the school?' he asked. 'Are ye enjoying teaching again?'

Eileen smiled as she answered. 'Yes, and it's one of the best ways of getting to know people.'

As she continued to talk, Alec was absorbed in not just what she said, but how she said it. He watched the light, graceful gestures she made with her hands, and the way her brown eyes lit up as she spoke enthusiastically of her students. He was quite content to listen to the pleasant tone of her voice, just nodding and laughing with her now and again. When Sam interrupted by bringing in the coffee, Alec had to make an effort not to scowl at him.

Sam put the tray on Alec's desk, nodded politely to Eileen, and left again, in a display of conspicuously good manners that didn't fool Alec for a moment.

There would be teasing ahead, once Eileen had left. In the meantime, though, he could make the most of her presence.

'How do ye like your coffee?' he asked.

The sheriff's office was lacking in fancy tableware but Sam had done his best with the tray. The coffee was in the regular, dented, ex-Army pot, with sugar in its usual tin, and some milk in an enamel jug. A worn silver spoon and two white china cups completed the set.

'A little milk and one spoon of sugar please,' Eileen said.

Alec served her first, then dumped two spoons of sugar into his own cup, leaving it black. He sipped it with satisfaction, then drew his attention back to his visitor.

'What brought ye here today?' he asked. 'Is there something I can do for you?'

'Yes, I hope so.' Eileen gazed at her coffee for a moment before looking up and meeting his eyes. 'I don't want to be a nuisance, but the miner who was bothering me, you remember?' When Alec nodded, she continued. 'He's still pestering me. Sometimes he's waiting not far from the school when I'm walking home.'

'Has he threatened ye?' Alec asked sharply.

Eileen shook her head. 'It's . . . I don't know if he's doing anything actually wrong, well, illegal. He just keeps on at me to have a drink with him, and he stands really close. I ask him to leave me alone but he won't.' Frustration was creeping into her voice.

'Has he followed ye home'?'

54

'Not that I know of. I don't go straight home when he's around. I go to the stores where he can't make too much of a nuisance pestering me. He gives up after a while.' She paused and sighed. 'I mentioned it to Mr Frampton, the headmaster; I thought he might escort me home or something, but he just said I should be pleased at the attention.'

Alec snorted. 'Frampton might be a headmaster, but he's no gentleman.'

'I've done my best to disencourage this Dench, but he won't take the hint,' Eileen went on, her hands clasped tightly around her coffee cup. 'I'm sorry to bother you with something so small, but I don't know many people in town, and I didn't know else to turn to. I suppose I should have gone to the town marshal—'

'I doan' mind ye coming here,' Alec told her, leaning forward. 'I'll make sure he – doesn't bother ye again, Mrs Wessex.'

The warmth of her smile was all the reward he could have wished for.

'I'll try and catch him outside the school on Monday, if he's there,' Alec promised. 'I'll be waiting to see him pester ye, just so I can swear to his behaviour in court if necessary, then I'll tell him if he doesn't quit bothering ye, I'll have his mangy hide.'

Eileen let out a soft sigh of relief. 'Thank you for being so understanding, Sheriff. I guess you must be really busy, with this second train robbery and all your other work.'

It was Alec's turn to sigh, this time in frustration. 'Arresting a miner for disturbing the peace will be nice and straightforward. I could do with something like that after chasing Al Donegan around the whole county.'

'Was it the same bandits who attacked both trains?'

'Seems like it, from the witness descriptions. They took both silver and gold this time, but at least no one got shot.'

'The same silver mine lost bullion again, didn't it?' Eileen asked, sipping her coffee.

'The Cornucopia, aye,' Alec agreed. 'The owner, Anderson, has increased the reward for information to two hundred dollars,' he added dryly.

'Two hundred?' Eileen repeated in surprise. 'Why, he must have lost thousands.'

Alec nodded. 'Anderson seems to be the kind who holds his money so tight he leaves fingermarks on it. He doesn't want to spend money even to increase the chances of getting money back.'

Eileen shook her head in disbelief. 'I wonder what the bandits are going to do with all that bullion? I'd have thought they'd had enough from the first robbery to last them a good while.'

Alec drank more of his coffee as he thought. That same question had occurred to him, rather vaguely, when he'd learned about the second robbery.

'It's not common for one gang to pull off two big robberies like that in such quick succession,' he agreed. 'Bullion isn't as easy to dispose of as cash. They'd have to be getting rid of it through a crooked banker, but I can't just go around asking to inspect bank vaults.'

Eileen finished her coffee and put the cup back on

the tray. 'I'm sure you'll catch them before long. I mustn't take up any more of your time, though.'

Alec stood up as she rose to leave. 'I'm glad ye came to me,' he said honestly. 'I'm glad to help.'

'Thank you.'

Alec escorted her through the outer office, occupied only by Sam at the moment. He held the door for Eileen, delighting in the light touch of her hand as she took his for a moment as they said good-byes. Then she was gone, walking away with a long, confident stride. Alec turned back into the office, and saw the sparkle in Sam's eyes.

'What did the lovely lady want?' Sam asked.

'She wanted help with a miner that's been pestering her,' Alec answered. 'And she asked me to pass on a message to you.'

'She did?' Sam sat upright, smoothing his dark hair back. 'I knew she was a woman of great taste.'

'She is,' Alec agreed, heading back to his own office. 'She said to tell you that your coffee is lousy.'

Karl Firth and Ethan Oldfield returned to Lucasville that evening. They had covered a lot of ground since leaving town the day before, and ate quantities of beef, potatoes and beans in the living quarters of the sheriff's building before settling down with coffee to report to their boss. The lawmen moved from the table to the mismatched collection of armchairs and rockers at the other end of the room. Each man had his own favourite chair. Karl used a red leather armchair that would have looked at home in a gentleman's club, just as Karl himself did. Sam sprawled in a chair covered in a faded floral chintz that stood out in the otherwise masculine atmosphere of the room. Ethan had a wooden rocker, softened with a colourful patchwork comforter, while Alec curled up in an oversized, wingbacked chair, that he particularly liked as he could rest his head against the high back, which also protected him from drafts.

'Well, ye didna find Donegan,' he said to Karl Firth. 'But did ye catch his scent at all?'

'We visited Caribou, Ward, Nederland and Sunshine,' Karl reported.

'I got another saddle sore for every camp and town we visited,' complained Ethan, making a show of rubbing his bottom.

'There was plenty of talk about the robberies,' Karl went on, ignoring the interruption. 'But we never saw hide nor hair of Donegan.'

'Ye learned something though?' Alec said, knowing Karl well enough to tell that there was more.

Karl looked thoughtful. 'When we were in Sunshine, we heard tell of someone up Pinewood Springs way who'd been seen spending plenty of money.'

'What's there to spend money on in Pinewood Springs?' Sam asked, swinging one leg as it hung over the arm of his chair. 'It's a plumb miserable mining camp, not even big enough to be called a town. Why, you could hire every whore in the place and still have change from twenty bucks.'

'That reminds me,' Ethan said. 'You borrowed twenty bucks off me last time you went up that way.'

Sam made an indignant face as Karl and Alec

58

chuckled. 'I don't need to spend money on whores,' Sam protested. 'Women like me so much they offer me money.'

'To stay away from them,' Alec said immediately.

When the laughter died down, Alec spoke to Karl again.

'Did ye learn anything more about the feller spending a heap of money in Pinewood Spring?'

'Just that a couple of men had been spending generously, buying the best whiskey, tipping the girls well, throwing plenty of money on the gaming tables, getting new clothes and acting as snappy as a pup with a new collar,' Karl explained. 'Rumour was they'd hit a new big claim, but no one could say for sure where it might be.'

'I haven't heard of any new claims being registered recent, but we could check the land registry office,' Alec mused.

'Ask around the haulage firms; see iffen they've taken machinery out to anyplace we ain't heard of,' Sam suggested.

Alec nodded. 'Good idea, but that's gonna take some time. I reckon you and I should ride up to Pinewood Springs tomorrow and see if we can catch up with these big spenders before they move on.'

'You want me to check with the land registry anyway?' Karl asked.

'Might as well,' Alec said. 'Maybe our train robbers are using a new mine as their front, making out the bullion came from their own place, when all they've got's a hole in the ground.'

'Smart thinking, boss,' Sam said.

'You better hope he's thinking just as smart when he runs you into trouble in Pinewood Springs tomorrow,' Ethan forecast gloomily.

Pinewood Springs was a patch of buildings huddled along the bottom of a long, V-shaped valley that rose into the Rockies. The air was rich with the resinous scent of the pines that clad the side of the valley, towering over and around the trail in a dark green mass, interspersed here and there with the purplish clumps of bare aspen that were still only just starting to show summer green, though it was now June.

Alec and Sam approached the town riding almost side by side, with Sam half a horse's length behind Alec. Sam rode his eye-catching paint mare, flashily marked with coppery chestnut and white patches. The mare carried herself with pride, ears pricked and her full, copper and white tail held high. Alec thought that she was a good match for Sam, so boyishly handsome, with his black frockcoat and multicoloured bandanna giving him a dashing air. There was more to both man and horse than mere show, however. Alec knew the flashy mare handled well and had plenty of stamina, and he knew well just how good Sam was with his twin guns, and how loyal he was.

Beside them, Alec felt himself and his horse to be distinctly plain. His own mount, Biscuit, was a pale dun, a creamy-yellow colour with fine brown mane and tail. He was as good as the paint mare, without being at all outwardly remarkable. As for himself, Alec Lawson preferred to wear straightforward clothes in unobtrusive browns and greens. He found nothing remarkable about his own face, or his dark-brown eyes and hair, considering himself rather ordinary. He remembered his mother telling him he was growing into a heartbreaker, but then mothers tended to be biased about their children. Alec smiled to himself at the memory, unaware that his mother hadn't been far wrong.

'Do we start searching in the saloon?' Sam's hopeful query broke into Alec's reverie.

'Might as well,' Alec agreed, looking about to see what had changed in the small town since his last visit.

Pinewood Springs was much like the other small mining towns scattered throughout Dereham County, and the Rockies in general. The buildings were mostly of lumber, some made of rough logs, and a few half-finished with tarpaulins. The most substantial buildings were the boarding houses for the mine workers, set back from the stores, saloons and banks that lined the main road through town. The town was busy in the late spring sunshine. Wagons were being loaded and off-loaded, a team of laden mules plodded through the muddy street, and dozing horses were tied in clusters to hitching rails.

Alec glanced about until he saw the fanciest saloon, and kneed his horse in that direction. They were looking for men with money to waste, so the Bon Ton Saloon looked like a good place to do that. It was later afternoon now, but he could hear music coming from the saloon, which seemed to be doing fair business.

'Should we get rooms here?' Sam suggested, glancing up at the windows of the first floor.

'Looks clean,' Alec answered, his attention more on the two men who had just left the saloon and were loading up their horses. He couldn't see them too clearly, as he and Sam were still some twenty feet away, and the men were half-hidden by the horses tied to the rail out front of the Bon Ton.

One man was having trouble with his bay horse, which was in a bad temper. The horse snorted and stamped a back leg as its girths were tightened. Alec heard a curse, and saw the horse flatten its ears in response to something, most likely a sharp dig in its belly. Its owner straightened up and flung a pair of heavily loaded saddle-bags behind the cantle of the saddle. The bay kicked out with one hind leg and swung itself round, barging into the man trying to fasten down the saddle-bags. He cursed again, and slapped the horse on its neck. The bay kicked out with both back legs, dislodging the saddle-bags. The leather bags flew sideways and landed on the street with a heavy clatter. One of the flaps hadn't been fastened properly and it burst open under the impact of landing, scattering small cloth bags into the muddy street.

Alec and Sam recognized the type of bag at once. They were the money bags used by banks. Alec's right hand dropped to his holster as he halted his horse.

'Hold it right there,' he ordered.

CHAPTER SIX

The man with the fractious bay froze for a long moment, staring at Alec. He was a scrawny, tow-headed individual, dressed in new range clothes. He didn't immediately resemble any of the men Alec had seen in the Caribou saloon. The bandit's pale blue eyes flickered as he rapidly considered his options.

'Bring your hands up where I can see them,' Alec ordered, his right hand resting on the butt of his Colt.

He kept his full attention on the nervous man half-hidden behind the bay horse. Alec didn't worry about the bandit's companion; Sam would be watching him. Slowly, the bandit raised his hands just enough that they showed over the horse's back.

'What's the trouble, Sheriff?' the scrawny bandit asked. 'It ain't illegal to knee your hoss in the belly iffen it blows itself out.'

'I doan' care about your horse,' Alec replied. 'I'm interested in what's fallen out of your saddle-bags. All those little banker's moneybags.'

The scrawny man swallowed. 'I . . . I work for a bank, Sheriff.'

'In that case, ye won't mind answering a few questions about which bank, and why you're carrying so much cash in your saddle-bags. Move out from behind the horse, and keep your hands up where I can see them.' Alec began to ease his Colt from its holster.

'Alec!'

Alec snatched his gun out and jerked sideways in the saddle at the same time. Two guns crashed, and horses squealed in fear, rearing and tugging at the reins that held them to the hitching post. Alec's horse shied, almost dumping him from the saddle. In the confusion, he lost sight of the scrawny bandit, but he didn't panic. Alec knew full well that he was a clear target mounted on his horse, so he kicked his feet from the stirrups and jumped down, landing on the side away from the bandits.

He was barely fast enough. As he dropped, he heard the slap of a bullet narrowly missing his head. Alec slapped his buckskin on the rump, to send it away from the shooting, and sprinted towards the horses tethered in front of the saloon. As he ran, he glimpsed Sam's riderless horse galloping further up the street, but continued gunfire reassured him that Sam had also dismounted to seek cover, and was keeping the second bandit busy. Alec dived between a grey and a roan, keeping his head down, and for once blessing his lack of height. The grey snorted and swung round, barging him against the roan mustang. Alec grunted at the impact, trying to keep his feet out from under the hoofs of the frightened horses.

'Take it easy,' he said quietly, running his free hand

along the horse's neck.

Without wasting time, he eased his way between the horses to the sidewalk in front of the saloon. All the time he was trying to see past the four horses that separated him from the scrawny bandit. Alec's mind worked fast and precise, with the inborn tactical ability that had kept him and his fellow soldiers alive through many combats. He weighed up the actions the bandit might take, and his own responses. Alec didn't want to get drawn into a long shooting match, as these two bandits could well have friends somewhere, which would change the situation and the odds against himself and Sam. He started by trying the bloodless option.

'Throw down your guns and surrender,' he called. 'There's no call for anyone to get hurt.'

The only answer was a defiant obscenity.

Alec didn't wait to hear more. Ducking under the hitching rail, he jumped on to the sidewalk and sprinted towards the bandit's position. Alec's boots thudded on the wooden boards, drawing the scrawny bandit's attention to his move, just as he'd calculated. He saw the bandit's head and shoulder appear, but the rest of the man was in the cover of his horse. Any shot Alec took that missed would hit either the bay or the frightened horse behind, and Alec couldn't bring himself to take that risk. By contrast, he was in clear view on the sidewalk, just a few feet from his enemy's gun. Alec twisted himself sideways, heard the crash of a gun firing and felt a blow against his side.

He cried out in pain as he fell, landing face-down in

a crumpled heap.

'Alec!' Sam heard his cry, and called anxiously from his position further along the front of the saloon.

Alec didn't move, even as the bandit scrambled up on to the sidewalk and approached him. The tow-headed man came within a couple of paces, peered down at the motionless sheriff, then took a step forward and kicked him in the ribs. Alec moaned softly, but did no more than half-open his eyes. The bandit snorted in satisfaction, and turned to help out his partner. He took just a couple of steps before he heard movement behind him. As he started to turn back, Alec snapped out a command.

'Drop the gun.'

Alec was sitting up, his Colt pointed steadily at the bandit, in spite of the patch of blood soaking into his shirt just above his waistband. The wound wasn't serious, barely a scratch, and he'd contrived to fall so the gun still in his hand had been hidden under his body. Now he had a clear shot at the bandit he'd lured on to the sidewalk, while the bandit's gun was pointed away from him.

The scrawny bandit's face flushed red with a mixture of anger and self-reproach.

'I knew I should've put some more lead into you!'

'Ye shoulda'stayed away from crime,' Alec replied. 'Drop the gun, carefully.'

The man stared at him for a long moment, fighting with his temper. Alec's Civilian Model Colt had a short barrel, but carried as much punch as the long-barrelled versions. At this range, it would throw a bullet clear through a man's head or body, leaving a bloody mess in its wake. The bandit moved his arm away from his body, tilting sideways, and let his gun slip from his fingers.

'Lean up against the wall,' Alec ordered, moving his head just enough to indicate the front of the Bon Ton.

Only when the bandit had obeyed did he climb to his feet, all the time keeping his gun trained on his prisoner. Alec had just got up when Sam bounded on to the sidewalk some fifteen feet away. His hat was missing, his hair was rumpled and there was dust smudged on his face, but on Sam, the effect was roguish, not messy.

'Alec! Why, you near on gave me a heart failure, making out like you'd been hit bad,' he said accusingly. As he moved closer, he also kept his gun aimed at the bandit.

'It worked,' Alec replied. 'Your man?'

Sam shook his head. 'Had to plug him in the chest. If there's a doctor in this town, he might be able to do something, or he's gonna die for sure.'

The scrawny bandit winced at Sam's words, but otherwise kept his expression still. While Sam kept him covered, Alec expertly searched and cuffed the bandit. With that done, Alec soon got the situation under control. The stolen money was picked up, the lawmen's horses recovered, the prisoner locked up in a storage shack and the dying man moved to a quiet bedroom in the saloon and made as comfortable as possible.

When everything was done, Alec sank down at a table in a corner of the Bon Ton with a cup of black coffee and a glass of whiskey. He took a long sip of the whiskey, letting the flavour fill his mouth before swallowing, then another. Then he poured half the remaining whiskey into his coffee.

'Is that wound bothering you?' Sam asked, leaning back in his chair at the other side of the table.

Alec shook his head. The bandit's bullet had scored a shallow furrow across his side, just above the waistband of his corduroy trousers. One of the doves at the saloon had bandaged it for him, and now it only really hurt if he moved incautiously.

'You sure don't look too pleased for a sheriff that's just caught a pair of bank robbers and recovered near on a thousand dollars cash,' Sam drawled.

'I was after train robbers, not bank robbers,' Alec answered, picking up his coffee and letting the scented steam warm his face.

When he'd questioned the bandit who'd surrendered, it had turned out that the two men had robbed a bank in Durango, and had fled north with their loot. The local sheriff had sent out wires about the robbery, but Alec had been thinking about Donegan when he'd followed the rumours to Pinewood Springs, not about a robbery that had taken place a month earlier at the other end of the state.

'Well, we done got bank robbers, whether we meant to or not,' Sam said. 'That's a good thing, as sure as God made little green apples. We'll haul them back to Lucasville tomorrow, lock one up, bury the other, and go right on looking for them train robbers.'

Alec sipped his coffee and looked across the table. Sam's easy-going, cheerful nature had been a help to him many a time when he felt under pressure, and his friend was doing his best to cheer him again. As usual, Alec felt some of the tension start to lift from his shoulders.

'You're right,' he said. 'We can go home tomorrow with one job well done, anyway.'

Thinking of Lucasville reminded Alec of his promise to help Eileen, and that thought finally made him smile.

Mid afternoon the next day, Alec left his office and headed through the outer office where his deputies were working.

'I'll be out for a couple of hours,' he told Karl, who nodded in reply.

Alec took just a couple of steps before Sam spoke up.

'Iffen that clock's right, school's not out for another hour yet.'

'Maybe the sheriff aims to get himself smartened up afore he plays gallant for the pretty schoolteacher,' Ethan suggested.

Alec glared at them as he walked towards the door.

'You-all reckon Alec's setting his cap for the lady?' Sam drawled, grinning.

'I notice that's a brand new shirt he's wearing right now,' Ethan commented, glancing at Sam, who nodded agreement.

'If ye haven't enough work to do, I need someone to take my saddle to the shop and get the stitching on the cinch rings repaired,' Alec said.

Ethan picked up his pen again, and Sam bent his

head over his papers. Just as Alec was closing the door after himself, he heard Ethan remark.

'Our sheriff sure gets mean when he's in love.'

Alec slammed the door, and promptly regretted it.

An hour later, he was carefully approaching the school where Eileen taught, keeping his eyes open for Tom Dench, the miner with the crooked nose. Just as Ethan had guessed he would, Alec had spent the last hour in the barber's shop, getting a shave and his hair trimmed. He'd considered cancelling, but couldn't think what else to do with himself until school was out, and eventually rebelled against the idea of letting his friends' teasing get to him. As he approached a possible confrontation with the miner, though, Alec became purely professional, concerned only with the job in hand.

Eileen had told Alec where the miner usually stood when he waited for her, so Alec approached the junction from a different angle. The school was set on a crossroads near the edge of town, where stores and houses intermingled. Dench usually waited outside a hardware store on the south-western corner of the crossroads, where he could easily see the school building on the south-eastern corner. Alec walked slowly from the north, strolling along a street of single-storey houses. Most of the traffic was heading east–west, on the street that cut across the one Alec was walking down. Wagons and drays rattled past, blocking his line of sight to the hardware store.

At least Alec had the consolation that if he couldn't see Dench, then Dench couldn't see him. When he reached the feed store on the north-west corner of the junction, Alec leaned against a water barrel and gazed thoughtfully towards the stores on the opposite side of the road. He admired a smartly turned-out buggy and team that trotted past, and when it was out of the way, he could see a figure lounging against the front wall of the hardware store. Alec couldn't see the man's face clearly, as he was staring at the front of the school, but his floppy hat and baggy, frayed jacket were familiar, and he wore a miner's denim pants and heavy boots.

There was no need for Alec to conceal himself; the miner never looked away from the school building. After watching the miner steadily for a couple of minutes, Alec let his attention wander a little as they waited for school to finish for the day. It wasn't often that he got to simply stop and watch the people he served going about their everyday business. An elderly couple were strolling together, enjoying the spring sunshine. A boy of about twelve emerged from the hardware store with his father, both laden with tools, wire and yard goods. They were talking cheerfully, maybe discussing whatever it was they were going to build together. A young woman with a baby wrapped in her shawl paused to look at the ribbons and fabric displayed in the window of a dry goods shop.

Lucasville seemed full of people living normal lives, families raising children and people going home at the end of the day. As he watched them, Alec found himself envying them. This current life, as a sheriff, was closer to everyday life than his ten years in the Army had been, but sometimes he still mourned the ordinary life he'd

71

had with his parents, before their deaths. Karl, Sam and Ethan were close friends, brought closer by the bonds that only shared dangers could create, but it was inevitable that eventually they would go their own ways. When he had the time to stop and consider himself, Alec sometimes felt hollow inside, an emptiness that needed a real family of his own to fill it.

In spite of his introspective mood, part of Alec's mind remained on alert. A movement from the figure across the street brought his attention sharply back to the matter at hand. Dench had produced a small flask from his pocket and was taking a drink. As Alec registered that action, he heard children's voices. School had finished for the day, and pupils were starting to leave. The first out were still struggling into coats and hats as they hurried away, chattering and laughing after the quiet of the classroom.

As the last stragglers left the school, Dench pocketed his flask and sauntered across the street. A few moments later, Eileen Wessex appeared, stepping lightly down from the entry porch. She saw the miner at once, and turned abruptly, heading east and away from Dench. He followed her, and Alec followed them both, pausing to let a delivery wagon pass. When he was free to cross the junction, he could see that Dench had almost caught up with Eileen, though she was walking briskly, schoolbooks tucked under her arm. Alec could hear the miner's voice, though he couldn't make out the exact words.

Alec stayed some twenty feet behind them, as Eileen continued walking, ignoring Dench's efforts to talk to her. She stared ahead, not looking at the heavyset man who was just behind her.

'Come on, Miss, it's plumb rude of you to ignore a man's talking to you,' Dench pleaded, his voice getting louder. 'I just want a little of your time.'

Eileen strode on, her body held stiffly with displeasure.

'I know this swell place where we can get a drink. It's got real imported wine.' The miner took told of Eileen's arm as he spoke.

Eileen whipped around. 'Take your hand off me!'

Alec hurried forward as Dench tightened his grip and started to pull at Eileen.

'Come on now. We can have a real good time together,' Dench urged.

'Let go!'

'Do like the lady says,' Alec warned, now just a few feet from them.

The crooked-nosed miner turned, still holding Eileen's arm, and glared at Alec. 'You butt out of this!'

Alec stood firm, staring back at the taller man. 'I've heard enough of this. Let go of her arm!'

Dench's eyes flickered downward to the gun at Alec's side; he slowly released Eileen's arm and turned to face Alec fully.

'I told ye once before to quit bothering decent women, and ye didna listen,' Alec said. 'I'm arresting ye on the grounds of being a public nuisance and disturbing the peace.'

Dench clenched his powerful fists, raising one at Alec, who let his right hand drift closer to his gun but took no other action.

'You've no right!' he bellowed, his face flushing red.

'I'm sheriff of this county, and I have the right.'

'There ain't no law saying who a man can talk to!' The miner's expression changed, becoming suspicious. 'You want me out of the way because you want her, don't you?'

The question caught Alec off guard for a moment. He certainly wasn't about to tell this man that he did like Eileen, but he didn't want to flatly deny any interest in her while stood right in front of her. After a brief hesitation, he spoke.

'What's important is what this lady wants. She doesna want you following her and pestering her, and she's said so clearly enough.' He drew his Colt with a fast, smooth movement. 'Put your hands against that wall and lean on them.'

Dench laughed harshly. 'You're a runty little hypocrite, Sheriff. You want her and you'll arrest anyone you thinks is trespassing on your territory.'

Alec bit down a fierce retort and gestured with his gun towards the wall. He was glad that the necessity of watching the miner meant he couldn't look at Eileen. When the man had been searched and cuffed, Alec turned to see Eileen watching, a slight smile on her face. Alec felt himself flushing as he caught her eye. He cleared his throat unnecessarily.

'I'll take this worthless cuss down to Marshal Clark's office and see the charges are brought against him,' Alec told Eileen. 'I saw him harassing you, so there's no need for you to be involved.'

Her smile widened. 'Thank you, Sheriff. I really appreciate your help.'

'He's just showing off to you,' Dench put in. 'He wants to make like a dime-book hero.'

'I wouldna have to rescue the lady if ye hadn't been bothering her,' Alec retorted. He hauled the miner away from the wall and turned him in the direction of the marshal's office. 'Now get moving.'

The miner turned his head for a last look at Eileen. 'I won't let him stop me.'

Alec gave him a hearty shove. 'Get moving!'

He took a quick glance at Eileen, seeing her smile at him again, then walked his prisoner off to the town marshal's office.

CHAPTER SEVEN

The locomotive's engine throbbed steadily as it waited at the station, almost as if the machine was breathing. Alec took a long, appreciative look at the coal-black 4-4-0 engine with its polished brasswork.

'That's a fine piece of engineering,' he remarked, reaching out to touch one of the massive drive wheels.

'You used to work on a railroad, didn't you?' Karl asked, standing beside him.

'I worked in a Chicago and Northwestern yard for about three years,' Alec told him. 'Started out as a wiper, greasing locomotives, then moved on to other jobs. I was an engine watchman for a little while, then a switch-engine fireman, and then a switchman for a few months, coupling the cars together.' He shook his head at the memories. 'Most dangerous job I ever had.'

Karl looked startled. 'Coupling cars together is more dangerous than the Army, or being a sheriff?'

'Sure.' Alec walked back along the train, to where the tender and the first boxcar were joined. He pointed to a flattened, tube-like object that projected from the bumper at the end of the car. 'That's the coupler pocket,' he explained.

Karl peered over his shoulder into the narrow gap between tender and boxcar.

'The link is what joins them,' Alec continued, indicating the metal coupling. 'It's just like a big link from a chain. Ye fit one end into the pocket on one car, and the other end into the pocket of the other car, and push a pin through the hole in each pocket to hold it in place.'

Karl could see there was very little room between the two cars. 'There's not much space to work in there.'

'Aye. Sometimes the pins wouldna' go in easily, or different cars would have coupling slots at different heights and you'd have to try an' find a gooseneck link that fitted. And when you got the link in one pocket, the engineer would back the other car up so ye could finish the connection.' Alec sighed. 'Many switchmen lost fingers or hands, crushed between the coupler pockets. An' I saw two men crushed to death between cars coming together. More than two died while I was working there. I just saw the two accidents: men getting caught between the bumpers.'

Karl considered the weight and size of the freight cars. Getting caught between two of them, even at a low speed, would be like getting crushed in a giant vice. 'I see why you thought the cavalry would be safer.'

'I always liked horses better anyway,' Alec answered. 'I wanted to leave the city.'

Which was something of an understatement. He'd grown to hate the noise and filth of the railyard. The accidents and deaths he'd witnessed had haunted his dreams. Joining the Army had become a way of escaping the city, and while it was still a risky occupation, Alec had felt that dying as a soldier was more worthwhile than becoming another railroad company accident statistic. Just a month before his twenty-first birthday, the age when he could enlist, a great fire had swept through the closely built timber buildings of Chicago. When it had finally died down, Alec had known for certain that he would leave the city behind as soon as possible.

Alec attempted to banish unhappy thoughts of the past by turning his attention firmly to the present. He straightened himself up and turned away from the train.

'We'd best go see what it is that Webb wants.'

They made their way across the busy station. A dozen or more buggies clustered together, waiting for passengers arriving on the next train. Wagons rumbled to and from the goods yard, piled high with everything from barrels of nails to crates of silk fabric. The smell of coffee and bacon drifted from the open windows of the dining hall that took up almost half of the depot building. Men and boys leaned on walls or perched on stacked goods, some hoping to earn a few cents by holding horses or carrying boxes, other just here to see whatever there was to be seen. There was an overriding smell of hot oil and metal, stronger even than the scent of men and horses gathered together.

Alec and Karl made their way through the throng to the depot building. Inside the ticket hall, Alec ignored the queues and made his way to the most senior clerk.

'Mr Webb asked me to see him,' he said.

The clerk saw the pointed-star badge on the lapel of his jacket and excused himself from his current customer.

'I'll let him know you're here, Sheriff.'

A couple of minutes later they were shown into the smart office of the railroad chairman. The lumber walls had been papered and all the furnishings were well made and expensive. Alec and Karl sat in a matched pair of elegantly carved walnut chairs, facing George Webb across his leather-topped desk. The air was full of the heavy scent of Webb's pipe tobacco; scrapings from the bowl were piled in a shallow silver dish to one side of the desk. In spite of his fancy office fittings and his well-made suit, George Webb still looked more like a labourer who swung pickaxe and mallet than the chairman of the railroad company.

He leaned forward in his chair, hunched and glaring like a boxer working himself up to a fight, and prodded a copy of the *Lucasville Trumpet* that lay on his desk.

'Lies!' he growled. 'Nothing but damn lies!'

Alec didn't need to be told which article Webb was referring to. The leading article and the editorial had been strongly critical of the Northern Colorado Railroad, questioning the policy of running valuable freight on the same train as passengers, and suggesting that once the railroad owners had taken money for passengers or goods, it didn't then take reasonable care of either.

'That's the second time that damned editor's dragged the Northern's reputation through the mud,'

79

Webb went on, glowering. 'I don't know why this O'Connell's doing this to me, but I want him to stop!'

'Have ye tried talking to him?' Alec asked reasonably.

Webb snorted like a maddened bull. 'What makes you think he'd listen to anything I have to say?' He picked up the paper and slapped it against the desk. 'This is what he thinks of me; this slanderous rubbish.'

'Libellous,' Karl muttered under his breath.

'If he is printing libel, you could sue him,' Alec suggested.

'I haven't the money to be wasting on lawyers,' Webb said. 'I want you to tell him to back down and quit riding me.'

Alec's eyes narrowed as he looked back across the desk at the sturdy man. 'Telling a newspaperman what to write isna part of my job,' he replied.

'You're paid to keep the peace, aren't you?'

'I'm not here to take sides in a dispute between businessmen,' Alec said firmly. 'The constitution upholds the right to freedom of speech.'

'He's trying to put me out of business,' Webb growled.

'The station looked busy enough,' Karl said. 'The mines and towns need the railroad to ship goods into the mountains, and the metal back again. Wagon teams and pack mules are just too slow.'

Webb sighed and leaned back in his chair. 'I know that. The articles are hitting the passenger trade mostly, especially the tourists. But these stories are shaking shareholder confidence in the company. A few have already sold up, so the value of the railroad company has dropped. The other shareholders get as nervous as a long-tailed cat in a room full of rocking-chairs, more sell up and the value drops again. When investors get panicky about a company, it sweeps through them like a town of prairie dogs diving for cover.'

'I'm sorry about that,' Alec said sincerely. 'But it really isna my job to be telling the editor of the *Trumpet* what he can print.'

Webb sagged, suddenly looking defeated. 'Have you got any closer to finding the men who robbed the trains?' he asked.

Alec shook his head regretfully. 'I wish I could. We know who we're looking for and I've wired the details to other sheriffs and the nearest US deputy marshals, so there's plenty on the lookout for them.'

'Thank you.' Webb nodded. 'I appreciate you taking time to come and see me, Sheriff.'

'I wish I could do more,' Alec answered, rising.

Karl rose as well. They made their goodbyes to the railroad manager, and went back out into the summer morning. As they walked back to the sheriff's office, Karl said, 'Maybe you should call on the newspaper editor, O'Connell, isn't it? I know you can't order him to quit writing about the railroad, but you might be able to talk some sense into him about it.'

'I may do,' Alec answered, glancing at a fine sorrel horse being ridden past. 'I don't want to get dragged into this mess, but it doesn't seem right to let a newspaper undermine confidence in a company and maybe make it go bankrupt.'

'You think that could happen?'

81

'I'm no expert on how shares and companies work, but Webb seemed plumb worried.' Alec barely knew George Webb, but the injustice of the situation nagged at him. 'I reckon the best thing I can do is find Donegan and his gang, and bring them to trial. It'll reassure folks that the railroad's safe to use.'

Karl glanced sideways at him, knowing how Alec's sense of justice would be driving him to resolve the problem. 'We'll catch them,' he said with calm confidence. 'You're a damn fine sheriff, Alec, and Donegan's going to find that out the hard way.'

Alec smiled back. 'We're a good team,' he admitted.

Alec pushed himself and his deputies hard in the search for Donegan. They went to the Land Registry Office and visited several haulage companies in an attempt to find new mines they hadn't heard of before. Acting on the information gained, they rode out to five new mines and three abandoned ones. Alec had wondered if a falsely registered claim, or a played-out mine was being used to pass off the stolen silver as legitimately produced. Miles of riding over mountain trails and talking to mine managers produced no results, except some resentment from a couple of miners who felt themselves accused of wrongdoing.

Alec also had to give evidence at the inquest into the death of the clerk who had been killed in the first robbery, and at the trial of a labourer he'd arrested weeks earlier for bludgeoning another man to death over a disputed card game. Two days later, he officiated at the labourer's execution. Alec hated hangings, though he believed execution was the only solution to some problems. Outwardly, he remained his calm, professional self, as the trapdoor fell away and the prisoner dropped through to choke his life away at the end of the rope.

While his regular duties were giving him enough to worry about, Alec saw Dench, the miner who had been pestering Eileen Wessex, hanging around near the sheriff's office. The first time, he was too busy to give the matter further thought, but over the next four or five days, he caught glimpses of that crooked-nosed face several more times. He half-expected to see Eileen in his office again, complaining about the miner, but she didn't come. Alec asked the town marshal, Tom Clark, if Eileen had been to see him, but Clark said she hadn't. Alec's feelings were mixed. He was pleased that Dench wasn't bothering Eileen any more, but selfishly a little disappointed that he didn't have a reason to get in touch with her again. Every time Alec saw Dench lounging on the sidewalk near his office, he felt more uneasy.

The room was thick with smoke. Alec woke, coughing, fighting to find air to breathe. From beyond his bedroom door, he could hear the crackle and roar of the flames that had already spread through the ground floor. Throwing back his blankets, Alec stumbled barefoot across the room towards the door. It was intensely, incredibly dark. With tears stinging his eyes, Alec groped for the doorknob, fear and despair building as he failed to find it. He was coughing, racking coughs that tore at his lungs as he fumbled with increasing desperation for the door knob. He had to get out! He had to warn his parents.

Alec's groping hand found the brass door knob and he grasped it regardless of the hot metal burning into his palm. He yanked the door open, and recoiled from the waves of heat that enveloped him. The stairwell was ablaze, gaudy orange light flickering through the rolls of smoke. Flames licked up the walls, the flowered wallpaper peeling and blackening at their touch.

'Ma!' The scream became a racking cough.

Alec clung to the doorframe, tears washing through the soot that blackened his face. He wanted desperately to reach his parents' room, to wake them and save them from the smoke and fire. But their room was at the head of the stairs, and flames were already spilling from the stairwell. If he tried to reach their door, the flames would sear his legs, turn his cotton nightshirt into a burning shroud.

The window at the end of the landing suddenly shattered, and the flames roared higher. Heat scorched his face, crisping and singeing his hair. Alec knew he should shut his bedroom door and climb out through the window. He knew how to escape, but terror held him paralysed. He was going to die like mother and father. A rolling wall of brilliant orange and red flame, curiously beautiful, surged towards him. Breathless in the suffocating heat, Alec felt his skin blacken and char.

He woke with a sharp moan, his heart thundering in his chest. Alec lay still for a few seconds, his hand clutching his pillow, then he curled up. A few tears squeezed out from his tightly shut eyes and long, groaning sobs tore themselves from him. After a minute or so, Alec had calmed enough to open his eyes and sit up. The curtains were half-open, allowing in enough light for him to dimly see the familiar shapes of his room in the sheriff's building. Alec shivered, and wiped his sleeve across his eyes.

He knew from bitter experience that he wasn't going to get back to sleep easily. He lit the candle on the little table beside his bed, comforted by the soft light even though it flickered like the flames in his nightmare. Pulling on a woollen dressing gown, Alec took the candle and padded quietly downstairs to the kitchen. He was standing by the stove, watching some milk warming in a pan, when a voice from behind made him jump.

'I hope there's enough in there for two.'

Alec whipped round, fear stabbing through him before his brain recognized Karl's voice, and he saw Karl's fair hair shining in the candle light. Karl held up his hand in apology.

'Sorry, Alec; I didn't mean to startle you.'

Alec took a deep breath, forcing himself to relax. 'I'm a wee bit jumpy.'

Karl nodded, his face sympathetic. 'You were dreaming about the fire again?'

'Aye. Did I wake you?' Alec asked anxiously.

'I heard you moaning and crying out,' Karl said gently. 'I don't think it was loud enough to disturb the others.'

Alec looked away, and saw that the milk was about to

boil over. He took the pan off the hot plate and divided the milk between two mugs. There wasn't much for either one, but it was warm and soothing.

Alec and Karl made themselves comfortable in their favourite armchairs, sitting in companionable silence as they sipped the hot milk. Alec was grateful for Karl's calm presence. He slowly sipped his milk and gradually relaxed, letting out a long sigh.

'Was it the usual dream?' Karl asked quietly.

'Pretty much, aye. I couldna' get to them an' I couldna' make myself escape. The flames came and burned me up.' Alec shivered.

His nightmare was of the fire that had killed his parents when he was fifteen. In real life, he hadn't panicked on seeing the flames cutting him off from his parents' room. He'd closed his bedroom door, thrown some clothes and a few belongings out of the window, and climbed out himself, hoping against hope that his parents had escaped too. Afterwards, the firemen had told him that his mother and father had died from the smoke, maybe even without waking, before the flames had reached them. No one had ever been able to say for sure how the fire had started, but it had left Alec orphaned and almost destitute, with his only family thousands of miles away in Scotland.

'Any idea why you had that dream?' Karl asked.

Alec thought about it. The nightmares had plagued him less frequently as time had passed. Now the fire dream only came when he was feeling pressured and worried.

'Trying to catch Donegan, hanging a man—' He

didn't mention repeatedly seeing Dench loitering near the office.

'It's been kind of busy,' Karl agreed, with characteristic understatement. 'Don't forget there's the dance next week. That's something to look forward to.'

Alec nodded, wondering if Eileen would be there. Which made him think of Dench again. Well, the hanging was in the past now, and he would keep working to find Donegan. But he knew where to find Dench. That was a worry he could tackle in the morning. Decision made, Alec suddenly yawned.

'Back to bed, I reckon,' Karl said.

CHAPTER EIGHT

Early the next morning, there was no sign of Dench loitering in the street near the office. Alec saddled his dun horse and headed up the trail to the Liberty Bell mine. He followed St Vrain Creek, climbing steadily up through the foothills towards Lyons. Once into the mountains, Alec turned south, making for Red Hill Gulch, the land growing wilder and more spectacular with every mile. Alec sat comfortably in his range saddle, enjoying the feeling of companionship with his horse as they picked their way along the forest trail. The horse's brown-edged ears flickered back and forth to the sounds of deer bounding away, or the trilling call of a waxwing. A spot of rusty-red caught Alec's eye, and he was delighted to see a fox curled up in a sunny clearing close to the trail, enjoying a nap.

The freshness of the air and his pleasure in the country he rode through, helped banish the lingering uneasiness of his nightmare. Alec was almost disappointed when he reached the Liberty Bell mine, which sprawled across a clear-cut section of the mountainside. He went to the company stable first, settling his horse in a spare stall, then headed to the main office.

'Hello, Sheriff, what can I do for you?' asked Kershaw, the superintendent.

Alec took the seat in front of the cluttered desk. 'I want to speak to Tom Dench.'

'Dench?' Kershaw shook his head. 'Sorry, Sheriff, he done quit on us a few days back.'

Frustration made Alec scowl. 'Goddamn it!' He yanked off his hat and rumpled his hair impatiently. 'I need to speak to him.'

Kershaw fiddled with his fountain pen. 'We were thinking of firing him, because he kept skipping shifts. Then he just upped sticks overnight.'

'Ye don't know where he went?' Alec asked.

'I don't,' Kershaw replied, unhappy at not being able to help someone.

Alec leaned back and thought for a moment. 'I saw him in Lucasville with some friends; would they know where he went?'

Kershaw's expression brightened. 'They might.' He tapped the end of the pen on the desk. 'Finn . . . Finn and Buckton. They're the two Dench used to pal up with.'

'Where are they? I want to see them,' Alec said, sitting upright.

Kershaw pulled over a piece of paper with a list of names on it. 'Ah . . . they're both down in the pit at the moment. I'll get someone to take you down.' He stood up, suddenly decisive. 'There's coffee on the heater.

Pour yourself some while I go fix things up.'

Alec nodded; he liked the idea of coffee more than he liked the idea of going down into the mine. But he really wanted to find Dench and resolve that worry.

Alec had never been inside a hoisting house before. He followed Symonds, the assayist, into the high-ceilinged lumber building, staring at the machinery. To his left were the steam-powered hoisting engines, three of them, each with its own engineer listening for the bell signals from below. Near the engines were huge spools of braided steel cable, each spool taller than Alec. One was moving as he watched, the cable unwinding itself smoothly as the machinery rumbled.

At the other end of the building, where the assayist, Symonds, was leading him, were the cages that dropped into the black hole of the mine shaft. Only one was currently visible, little more than a simple open-sided iron frame. Pipes snaked across the floor and vanished down the sides of the shaft. Alec picked his way carefully over the metal car rails inset into the wooden floor, and halted beside the assayist.

'These cages drop pretty fast,' Symonds said, passing Alec a candle. 'Don't stick your arms, your head, or anything else you want to keep, outside of the frame. Anything hits against a timber, you'll lose it, messily.'

'Aye,' Alec answered, wondering just how urgently he wanted to talk to Dench's pals. Well, he'd come this far: Alec stepped into the cage beside the shabbily dressed assayist.

A few moments later, the cage began to drop and

Alec's stomach seemed to lurch into his mouth. He swayed, grabbed for the frame to steady himself and then remembered the warning. He glanced round, and saw that Symonds was holding on to the frame, and felt a little better. They were swallowed in darkness, lit only by their candles and glimpses of lamplight from levels as they passed by. The cage descended far faster than Alec had thought possible, causing him to glance anxiously upwards, wondering about the cable that held them. He was immensely relieved when the cage finally halted.

'The men you want are on this level,' Symonds said, apparently unmoved by the experience.

Alec followed the stolid assayist into the tunnel. Lamplight helped the weak light of their candles, thrown back from the rock walls in a myriad of glittering points. Sounds of machine drilling echoed from ahead, almost drowning the drip of water from somewhere. Alec had imagined the mines would be cold, but instead the air was hot, almost uncomfortably so.

'Is that the ore reflecting the light?' Alec asked.

Symonds shook his head. 'Quartz.' He plodded onwards.

Alec had no idea how far underground he was, and didn't really want to know. There was no daylight here, not even the faint light of stars and moon he was used to at night. They were completely and utterly surrounded by rock. The only way out was via that cage and its steel rope. Alec took a deep breath, fighting down the feeling of being trapped, and concentrated on picking his way along the level. The sound of drilling grew louder, booming around in the tunnel to a point Alec found painful.

He was grateful when the noise stopped, just before they reached the working face. There, in the yellow lamplight, he recognized the two men he'd seen with Dench the time he'd first met them pestering Eileen. Down in the mine they were working shirtless, their torsos shining with sweat, though both men wore shapeless hats to keep the worst of the dirt out of their hair. One man was changing the drill bit on the compressed-air drill, while the other was scraping rock dust from the new hole with a long-handled copper spoon. They paused in their work on seeing visitors, and put down the equipment to approach when Symonds beckoned to them.

This was their territory: the miners were at home here, in this dimly lit, rock-enclosed world so far below the surface of the earth. Though Alec had forced them to back down before, they approached now with confidence. Alec knew he was the outsider in this world, but he concealed his discomfort, straightening up and facing the two taller men boldly.

'I need to know where Dench is,' he said.

The two miners looked at one another.

'Don't rightly know where he's at,' Buckton drawled. 'Ain't seen him in a few days.'

'Did he take his kit with him?' Alec asked.

'He surely did.' Finn folded brawny arms across his chest. 'Tom said as you're out to get him, Sheriff.'

Alec made an exasperated sound. 'I just want him to

quit bothering Mrs Wessex.'

'You want Tom outta the way so's you can chase her yourself,' Finn said.

'That's not it!' Alec took a deep breath. 'She came to me, complaining about his behaviour. I'd arrest any man for pestering any woman that didna want his attention.'

'Tom don't think that,' Buckton drawled. 'He reckons you're chasing her too, and he said he was gonna stop you.'

'Stop me how?'

Buckton shrugged. 'He just gave out how he wasn't going to let some half-grown sheriff stop him from getting his woman.'

Finn gave a grunting laugh. 'Tom said he could beat the tar outta you as easy as licking butter offen a knife.'

'He reckoned he could beat me?' Alec asked.

Finn nodded. 'He sure did. Tom reckoned by the time he'd finished with you, you'd be as ugly as a tar-bucket, and no woman in town would be interested in you.'

'I'm plumb surprised you're walking now,' Buckton put in. 'Tom ain't the kind to let grass grow under his feet.'

This was the information that Alec had really wanted: confirmation of his suspicions about why Dench was watching him instead of Eileen.

'Ye both heard him say he was going to attack me?' Alec asked, speaking clearly enough to be heard by Symonds too.

Both miners smirked at him. 'Sure did.'

93

Alec suddenly grinned, enjoying the look of surprise on their faces. 'Then you're both witnesses to the fact that Tom Dench has threatened to attack me. So if he does try anything, I can show it was premeditated.'

Finn and Buckton glanced uneasily at one another, realizing they'd been trapped.

'Well, now—' Finn started.

'You heard all that, didn't you, Symonds?' Alec asked.

'Sure did,' answered the assayist.

Finn glowered at the sheriff while Buckton clenched his powerful hands into fists, but neither of them could find anything to say.

Alec grinned at them again. 'I'll not keep you any longer. Thanks for your help.' He nodded to them, and turned to start the long journey out of the mine.

On his way back to Lucasville, the pleasure of the ride only partly diverted Alec from his thoughts about Dench. By the time he reached the stable out back of the sheriff's office, he had made up his mind that he had to get Dench to leave town. He was certain that the miner would refuse to go, but Alec wanted to give him the chance of leaving without trouble. Alec unsaddled his horse, leaving it with a pat and a generous feed, and entered the law building through the kitchen door. Only Karl was in the front office, reading a copy of the municipal laws.

'Did you learn anything?' he asked as Alec entered.

'Enough. Is Dench out there?' Alec nodded towards the front window.

'He was earlier.' Karl stood up and looked out. 'Yeah; he's in his usual place.'

'Good. Stay in here, but watch out for me, all right?' Alec spared Karl a brief glance as he headed across the room to the door in the centre of the front wall.

'Yes, ss—' Karl narrowly bit off the 'sir' he would have added in their army days.

Alec headed across the street, making no attempt to hide his intention. He saw Dench straighten up, and slip his penknife and the wood he'd been whittling into the pocket of his baggy jacket. There was a slight smirk on the miner's unshaven face that reminded Alec uncomfortably of his threats. None of the sheriff's inward doubts showed on his face as he stopped in front of the taller, stronger man.

'Dench, I'm telling ye to move on; leave Lucasville,' he said firmly.

Dench folded his arms. 'And what law lets you tell me where I can stay? This is a free country.'

'Ye've no job and you're sleeping rough. By the laws of this town, you're a vagrant, and I have the authority to arrest you or throw ye out of town.'

Dench's face flushed with anger. 'There's other men sleeping rough in this town, and you ain't chasing them away.' He pointed a finger accusingly at Alec. 'You're just using your office to get rid of me, 'cause you're scared of me. You want that schoolteacher too, and you want me out of the way.'

Alec's temper started to rise too. 'I already told ye, what I want makes no difference. I'm concerned with what Mrs Wessex wants, and she doesna' want ye bothering her.'

'But you do want her, don't you?' Dench accused. 'You've set your cap for that pretty widow; I seen the way you looked at her.'

'Are ye gonna start moving or do I have to force ye?' Alec demanded, lowering his right hand towards his gun.

'You're not man enough.' Dench lunged forwards, his hands shooting out to shove Alec backwards.

Alec had been expecting a punch, not a straightforward shove to his chest. He staggered back, off balance, and caught his bootheel on one of the uneven boards of the sidewalk. It was enough to ruin his balance altogether and Alec fell, arms windmilling. He landed painfully on the base of his spine and collapsed on to his back. Dench rushed at him, yelling, his foot drawn back to deliver a kick with his heavy boot. Alec twisted aside, his holstered gun digging uncomfortably into his hip as he rolled over it. Dench's boot hit his thigh but not hard enough to injure.

Alec kept rolling and scrambled sideways to the edge of the sidewalk. He let himself drop to the packed earth of the street, landing on his back. As Dench jumped down after him, Alec sat up and managed to draw his Colt.

'Surrender! You're under arrest.'

For a moment, he thought that Dench was going to keep on coming. Then the miner stopped, fists clenched and face flushed.

'You low-down skunk!' Dench yelled. 'Iffen I ever catch you without your iron, I'll clean your plough but good. Your own mother won't recognize you when I've done. I'll fix you so no woman will ever look at you again.'

Alec picked himself up carefully, never taking his eyes or his gun from the furious man.

'I'd surely say that sounds like threatening behaviour,' said Karl, appearing alongside him, with his gun also drawn.

'Good timing,' Alec commented gratefully. 'Cuff him and we'll take him to the marshal's office.'

He watched with quiet satisfaction as Karl fitted the metal cuffs to Dench's wrists. He hadn't been able to get Dench locked up before for pestering Eileen, but he had enough now to keep the miner behind bars for a while.

With the problem of Dench out of the way, Alec's spirits rose. He hadn't got any closer to finding Donegan, but at least no more trains had been robbed by the time the Lucasville Foundation Dance came around. This was one of the big social events of the year, held to celebrate the anniversary of the city's charter being granted. The largest dancehall was taken over for the night and redecorated by the Women's Civic Committee in a style more suitable for an important civic occasion.

The guests were also dressed up to match the event. Alec still had his smaller revolver in an inside pocket of his black suit jacket, but his gun-belt was back in his bedroom. The sound of a spirited polka filled the warm air as he mingled with the other non-dancers at the edge of the hall. Alec rather liked dancing, but tended to be self-conscious about it. Sam had no such inhibitions, and was out on the dance floor now, whirling a pretty red-haired girl about the floor with style. Ethan was also dancing, though with less flair, and Karl was talking with Renee Winter, the sister of one of Lucasville's banker owners. Karl and Miss Winter had been courting quietly and steadily for some months.

Alec watched them for a few moments, then turned his attention to the rest of the room. It took him a couple of minutes to find her, but when he saw Eileen Wessex, a smile lit up his face. She was wearing an elegant dress of dusty pink, trimmed with cream lace. Her hair was braided and coiled into a large mat that covered the back of her head. The light of the oil lamps added highlights that shifted as she turned her head. Eileen was talking to a man Alec vaguely recognized from the Land Registry Office. Alec sipped his beer and enjoyed just looking at her.

He vaguely noticed that the polka had finished, being more engrossed in studying the relationship between Eileen and the Land Office man. She was listening politely to him, smiling now and again, but sometimes she glanced around the room as he was talking to her. The caller announced the next dance, and the Land Office man held his hand out to Eileen, clearly inviting her to dance. Alec frowned, then felt a sudden joy as she shook her head. He couldn't hear her through the chatter around them and the sound of bootheels on the lumber floor, but she was making some apology for her refusal. Alec wondered why she didn't want to dance, and started to worry. As he stared through the crowd at her, Eileen looked around the room again, and her gaze met his. Her face brightened in a smile and she began to squeeze through the crowds towards him. Alec smiled too, and moved to met her.

After the first greetings, Alec asked her if she was enjoying the dance.

'Why, yes,' she replied warmly. 'I've been that busy with school duties, and not liking to go out on my own while Dench was about, that I've not had much opportunity to make new acquaintances. I heard you arrested Dench?'

Alec nodded. 'He tried to knock me into next week, so he's now waiting trial on charges of assault. I don't think he'll be able to post bail, so he'll be behind bars till he comes to trial, and then for a while afterwards.'

'I'm surely grateful to you for listening to me,' Eileen told him.

'It's what any decent man would have done,' Alec said sincerely.

Eileen smiled. 'In any case, I feel much safer now, and I plan to join one or two societies.'

'What did ye have in mind?'

'I aim to join the Lucasville Musical Society,' Eileen said. 'I play the flute and the piano. Are you musical, Mr Lawson?'

'Please, call me Alec,' he said impulsively. 'I'm afraid I don't play any instrument. I enjoy listening to music but I don't know much about it.'

'Enjoyment is the most important aspect of music,' Eileen said. 'Like enjoying this waltz they're playing.' She glanced at the colourful crowd of dancers. 'Oh,

Alec, do you know who that man is?'

Alec looked at where she was pointing. 'Do ye mean the long-faced man with the moustache?'

'Yes, dancing with the woman in the fringed blue and pink dress.'

'That's Anderson,' Alec said. 'He owns the Cornucopia Mine that had bullion stolen in the train robberies. Why d'ye ask?'

'He almost knocked me over a little while ago. He came hurrying out of the newspaper office and ran straight into me. He did apologize,' Eileen added.

Alec looked at Anderson, who was bowing to his wife as the dance ended, and wondered briefly what he'd been doing in the newspaper office. Eileen's company was far more interesting, though, and curiosity about Anderson was soon forgotten.

'Have you got any further in finding the men who've been stealing the bullion?' Eileen asked. 'You were on the first train they robbed, weren't you?'

'I was,' Alec admitted. 'Along with Sam.'

Alec told Eileen about that robbery and found himself talking more about the search for the outlaws. She listened intently, asking intelligent questions now and again. Alec found it a relief to be talking about the problem to someone who wasn't one of his deputies, or a demanding party like Anderson. He found himself talking easily to Eileen Wessex. She was interested, but his decisions didn't affect her life in the way that his deputies' lives depended on his ability to make the right choices.

'I've talked plenty about myself,' he said at last,

searching her face for signs of boredom. 'I should let you talk.'

'There isn't much to say about my life,' Eileen protested.

Alec wanted to disagree: he wanted to know more about her. What books she liked to read, whether she liked horse riding, whether she laughed at the same things he did. He smiled at her, wondering what to ask first, and realized that a dance had just finished and the caller was urging couple to take to the floor. Alec started to lift his hand and opened his mouth to speak, on the point of asking her to dance with him. Then the knowledge came crashing in that she was a widow: that she was mourning her husband. He snapped his mouth closed and swallowed. Eileen didn't speak, clearly waiting for him to say something.

Alec abruptly lifted the glass in his other hand.

'I need a drink. Can I get you anything?'

Eileen's expression became inscrutable. 'I'm fine, thank you,' she said politely.

'Good,' Alec replied automatically. 'Please excuse me.'

He turned away from her, heading first for the bar, then veering away. Eileen had clearly guessed what he'd intended to ask, and she'd been offended. Alec cursed himself under his breath as he made his way through the crowd.

'Alec?'

Alec stopped short, finding Karl alongside.

'Are you all right?' Karl asked.

Alec sighed. 'I reckon so. I've had enough for this

101

evening; I'm going to walk round town a little and then go home,' he added.

'Will you be all right on your own?'

Alec nodded. 'You stay with Miss Winter and enjoy yourselves. If ye want something to do, you can keep an eye on Sam and Ethan for me.'

Karl gave a mock shudder. 'Those two are old enough and ugly enough to know what they're doing. Good night, Alec.'

'Good night.' Alec nodded to his friend and headed out alone to the cooler night. He felt calmer outside, though still annoyed with himself for letting his feelings for Eileen Wessex show so clearly. In the future, he had to remember that she was a widow, and that she didn't want to be pestered by men. He needed to stop thinking of her, and to start thinking more about the train robberies.

CHAPTER NINE

The office of the *Lucasville Trumpet* was full of the rattle and thump of the week's edition being printed. Thinking back on his encounter with Eileen Wessex the night before, Alec remembered her comment about Anderson bumping into her as he left the newspaper office. Anderson's clumsiness suggested that the mine owner had had something on his mind, and Alec wondered what that might be. Why it should be relevant, Alec didn't know, but some instinct told him that there was more to Anderson than there seemed. Something about the man didn't seem quite right, and Alec was determined to find out more.

As he waited, Alec watched, fascinated, as the printers deftly fed clean sheets into the machines and drew out neatly printed copies. He only had a couple of minutes to enjoy the smooth flow of the processes before he was ushered into the editor's office. O'Connell came to his feet as Alec entered, straightening his back and shoulders. Alec spotted the

103

upswing of the editor's hand that was about to become a salute before being changed to a handshake.

'I'm pleased to meet ye,' he said, shaking O'Connell's firm hand before taking a seat.

'And you,' O'Connell replied, smiling from under his droopy moustache. 'How are you making out, looking for Donegan?'

Alec shrugged. 'We're following up every lead we get. I'd sure like to get my hands on him, but this is a big country and we can't be everywhere at once.'

'I'm sure you'll catch up with the son-of-a-bitch sooner or later,' O'Connell said, with more confidence than Alec sometimes felt. 'You ain't no quitter.'

'I'm glad you think so,' Alec replied, relaxing back into his chair.

O'Connell nodded, then sucked loudly on his teeth. 'I remember hearing about you, Captain Lawson. The men who made it up from private to commissioned office like you, are scarcer than hen's teeth. And them deputies you got, they was with you in the army, weren't they?' He didn't give Alec the chance to answer. 'I'd say that's the mark of a good officer, when his men keep on working with him even when they don't have to.'

Alec smiled, a little embarrassed, but pleased by the newspaperman's comments. 'I'd guess you've seen service yourself?' he said.

O'Connell nodded. 'Sure did, though nothing like you. I made sergeant in the infantry, mostly 'cause I was a trained carpenter.'

Alec nodded. 'They'd have plenty of use for a man with a skill in his hands. I could have used one myself sometimes, when they set us to fixing up bridges and the like.'

'I'll guess that's not what you joined the cavalry to do.'

'Well, no,' Alec admitted. 'But I was always interested in building things, that kind of engineering. Though I swear ye could have tiled roofs with the hardtack they used to give us.'

O'Connell laughed. 'It wasn't only the uniforms they had left over from the War Between the States.'

The two men spent a little while reminiscing about their experiences in the army, and especially about the horrors of the food they'd been served. Alec was pleased to find it was so easy to find something in common with O'Connell, but never forgot his purpose in making the visit. As the initial chat faded, Alec remarked, 'I've been reading your articles in the *Trumpet* about the North Colorado Railroad.'

He watched O'Connell as the weathered face changed expression.

'You've no' been kind to the railroad,' Alec added.

O'Connell sucked on his teeth. 'There's been two hold-ups recent, and a heap of silver been taken.'

Alec nodded in acknowledgement. 'I ken. And I've got no beef with ye reporting on that. But what you've written is making the railroad look real bad. The shareholders are getting jittery, and Webb, the owner, is running into trouble on account of it.'

O'Connell stared defiantly across the desk. 'Webb's got a railroad to run; I got a newspaper. I got to shift copies, and get subscribers. If folks want to read about a railroad that ain't looking after them right, then I'm gonna tell them about it.'

Alec sat straighter in his chair, losing the relaxed pose and becoming more like the officer he'd been. 'I heard tell that Anderson was in here the other day, and I know he doesn't advertise in your paper. He's got a for-real grudge against the North Colorado too, just like you seem to.'

O'Connell looked down at the desk.

'Is there any connection between Anderson visiting, and you badmouthing the North Colorado in your paper's?' Alec asked sharply.

O'Connell responded by straightening his shoulders again, coming to attention at the sound of an officer's voice. He gazed past Alec, without meeting his eyes.

'I asked ye a question,' Alec snapped.

'Anderson wanted me to make the article stronger,' O'Connell admitted.

Alec snorted impatiently. 'Did he now?' He studied the editor for a moment, seeing how uncomfortable the man was. 'And did he want it enough to pay ye for it?' he asked in sudden inspiration.

O'Connell nodded. 'The paper needs more subscribers, and he wasn't asking me to tell downright lies; just to exaggerate things.'

'So ye took his money to print harsh words about a man who's never done ye any harm.' Alec didn't have to fake his scorn. 'I guess that's a matter between you and your conscience. I saw Webb the other day and he told me that if he read any more articles in your paper badmouthing the Northern Colorado, he'd be calling

106

in his lawyers and sueing you. Ye might want to consider that next time Anderson asks ye to write his words.'

O'Connell made himself meet Alec's gaze. 'There's nothing I'd rather do than run my own newspaper. When you want something very much, you do things you wouldn't do other times.' He paused. 'I'll ... remember what you told me about Webb sueing if I write more.'

Alec nodded, sorry at having put O'Connell in this position, but keeping his feelings to himself.

'Thank ye for telling me the truth,' he said. 'Did Anderson say why he wanted you to write those articles?'

O'Connell shrugged his brawny shoulders. 'He talked some about you, said he'd just been to see you, then talked about how the Northern Colorado should take better care of the goods and passengers it carried. I guess he wants the railroad to have a bad name in case he decides to sue them for the bullion he lost.'

'If the Cornucopia and the railroad want to set into fighting one another, you'd be best to stay out of it,' Alec advised. Picking up his low-crowned hat, he rose and bid the newspaperman farewell. 'I hope next time we meet, we can be friends.' Alec held out his hand.

O'Connell took Alec's hand in his own broad one and shook it. 'You're doing your job, Sheriff, and I appreciate that.'

Alec left at a brisk walk, slowing down once he was outside in the sunshine. As he made his way back to the office, he pondered on what he had learned. He'd got the distinct impression that Anderson was tight with his money, so why was the mine owner spending cash on bribing O'Connell to criticize the railroad? Those same articles were bringing the railroad close to bankruptcy. If Anderson sued, Webb wouldn't be able to pay him anything worthwhile. Alec wondered if there was some personal history between the two men. It would bear looking into, he decided.

Anderson handed his hat and coat to the maid, and walked briskly into his parlour, settling himself on his leather armchair. His wife, Pearl, looked up from her fashionable magazine. This room, and the dining room, were the most stylish in the house, worthy of a well-to-do mine owner. Pearl had stayed within the budget he'd allowed her, and her sure taste showed in the elaborately swagged curtains, the beaded lamps and the quality of the runners and doilies that layered the mahogany furniture. Pearl herself fitted the house, with her blonde curls, and stylish dresses, modelled on those in the magazines. It was a home life that Anderson felt any man should be proud of.

'Are you all right?' Pearl asked, her voice carefully modulated and ladylike.

'I met O'Connell, the newspaper man, on my way home this evening,' Anderson told her.

'Does he want more money?' Pearl asked.

Anderson shook his head. 'It seems the sheriff was in his office yesterday, asking about those anti-railroad articles. Lawson got it out of O'Connell that I'd paid him to write those articles. O'Connell says he won't do any more; no more.'

Pearl closed her magazine and placed it on the small table beside her chair.

'Has the sheriff spoken to you about it?'

'No. No,' Anderson repeated. 'I was hoping I wouldn't have to do it, but I reckon I'll have to ... entice ... Lawson, anonymously; just enough to keep him sweet. That's why I want you to invite him to dinner tomorrow, or the day after,' he went on. 'I want him to see this.' Anderson gestured at the room they were in. 'And want some of it for himself.'

He stopped there. While Pearl knew he'd been trying to weaken the position of the railroad via the newspaper, she didn't know about his other schemes. She'd never shown any interest in knowing where his money came from, so long as he could provide wealth and the social status she believed went with it.

'If he hasn't done anything about O'Connell taking money to write your articles about the railroad,' Pearl said thoughtfully, 'he probably doesn't see anything too wrong in taking money himself. Not over something like businesses squabbling and sueing one another.' She glanced around the parlour, smiling with pride. 'I bet he'd like some money to spend on fancy food and fittings as fancy as this.'

Anderson smiled, revealing his rather prominent teeth. 'I want you to put on a good show for him, Pearl, a good show.'

She nodded. 'I'll have to invite someone else; maybe Winter and his sister. It'll look odd if Sheriff Lawson's the only guest.'

'Whatever you think is suitable,' Anderson told her.

He had full confidence in Pearl's ability to organize the social side of things. She would impress the sheriff with the good things that money could bring, and charm him. Then Lawson would be all the more susceptible to Anderson's money. The mine owner reminded himself of just how much money he calculated his plan would bring, and was satisfied that bribing a sheriff was a worthwhile expense.

The morning after the Anderson's dinner party, Alec was, for once, the last one down to breakfast. Sam grinned at him as he sat down somewhat heavily at the table.

'You had a swell night then?' he asked.

Alec scowled at him. 'I doan' have a hangover. It's been a while since I last ate that much rich food.' He gave Ethan a nod of thanks as the taller man set a mug of fresh coffee in front of him. The steam from the coffee caressed his face, soothing the mild headache that Alec didn't feel worthy of the description 'hangover'. He'd done his share of hard drinking as a soldier, though with beer and whiskey. He didn't have much experience with wine, especially the fine sort that went down effortlessly, like he'd been offered the night before.

His remark about the food was true though. The Andersons had put on a fine spread, served by the maid, and they'd eaten off a table swathed in lace-edged linens. Alec had felt daunted by the array of silver cutlery set out at his place, but he'd remembered his days in the officers' mess, and had managed without embarrassment.

'What did you have to eat, then?' Sam asked, tucking into his own breakfast of ham, eggs and hot biscuits.

'Oyster soup with crackers.' Alec paused to sip his coffee. 'Duck with rice. Roast beef with potatoes, creamed vegetables and gravy. Rice pudding and orange sponge jelly.'

Ethan sighed. 'Why don't we eat like that, boss?'

'Any time ye learn to cook that kind of thing, we will,' Alec answered.

'Cain't we hire a cook?' Sam suggested. 'A pretty one, with red hair?'

'Did you learn any more about Anderson?' Karl asked Alec, ignoring Sam.

That was the important question: the reason why Alec had accepted the invitation. He'd wanted to learn more about the mine owner, hoping to get an idea of why Anderson had been paying out for anti-railroad articles in the *Trumpet*. Alec drank more of his coffee and considered his answer.

'He's no' short of a few pennies,' Alec said slowly. 'His parlour and dining room are mighty fine rooms; carpets, good furniture, silver candlesticks, that kind of thing. His wife had some fancy jewellery on.'

'Pretty lavish, eh?' Sam suggested.

Alec almost agreed, then shook his head. 'Not lavish, quite. Very nice and comfortable, the kind of home any man would be proud to have. But not extravagant.' He paused, trying to work out what it was he'd felt about Anderson's home.

There was a bang on the front door of the building. Ethan was nearest, so he sighed, got up, and went through into the office.

'It was like Anderson wanted to put on a good show, but couldn't quite bring himself to spend the money. The finishing touches weren't quite there.' Alec frowned, and took another drink. 'I can't put my finger on it.'

'Your instincts are usually pretty good,' Karl said. 'I reckon you're close to it; Anderson was putting on a show; he wanted to impress you. The question is, why?'

'Maybe he's trying to make you a friend so you'll work harder at catching whoever's done stolen his silver?' Sam suggested, gesturing with his fork.

'He doesn't know Alec very well, if he thinks that'll work,' Karl retorted.

Sam shrugged. 'I never said it would work, just that Anderson might think it would.'

Ethan returned from the office and held a plain envelope out to Alec.

'Someone had pushed this under the door,' he explained. 'There's probably a mousetrap inside,' he added, as Alec pulled open the envelope and reached inside.

Alec ignored this, and withdrew a letter on plain, good-quality paper, and a wad of notes. He read the letter swiftly, his eyebrows drawing down as anger flashed in his eyes. His three deputies recognized the signs, and glanced at one another, waiting for the outburst. Alec shoved the letter across the table to Karl, and stood up so abruptly his chair fell over. He paced back and forth in short strides as Karl read the letter, with Ethan peering over his shoulder. Sam picked up the money and counted it.

'. . . the matter of the Northern Colorado Railroad is a purely business concern . . .' Karl read aloud.

Sam whistled. 'Seven hundred dollars!'

'A bribe!' Alec snapped, rolling his r's and lapsing into a Scottish accent so strong it took his deputies a moment to understand what he'd said. 'A damned bribe!'

Karl picked up the envelope and was studying the writing on that and on the letter.

'There's no signature,' he said.

Alec halted his pacing to glare across the table. 'It hasta be Anderson. There's only Anderson, Webb and O'Connell involved in this dispute about the railroad, an' neither Webb nor O'Connell have the money to be spending on a bribe.'

'Anderson showed you the kind of money he has last night,' Karl commented.

'Aye.' Alec took a deep breath, forcing himself to calm down and start thinking. 'That's why he invited me to his house. He wanted me to see that he has the money to make a payment like that.'

'Do we arrest him now, or after breakfast?' Sam asked, his eyes shining with eagerness.

Alec shook his head. 'We don't have proof Anderson sent that letter. I'm willing to bet it was him, but there's nothing that would convince a jury.' He picked up his chair and sat down again. 'Karl, I want you to keep hold of that money until I decide what to do with it. There's good causes will be pleased to see some of that, but I need a few days to choose how much goes where. If anyone can show that I've been keeping hold of it myself, it could look like I've accepted the bribe, no matter that I was intending to give it away.'

Karl nodded, and prised the money from Sam's fingers, returning it to the envelope.

Alec wrapped his hands around his coffee mug, as though trying to warm himself after the cold ugliness of the bribe, and stared into the dark liquid. Sam caught Ethan's eye, and shook his head in mock sorrow for Anderson. The mine owner had just made a big mistake.

CHAPTER TEN

By mid afternoon, Alec's temper was still simmering like a kettle on the edge of a stove. The initial outrage over the bribe had subsided, but repeated frustration was stoking the heat. The morning had brought a mass of paperwork, mostly involving taxes or applications for licences for everything from brothels to liquor stores.

Immediately after a hasty lunch he'd appeared in court to give evidence in the trial of a carter who'd strangled a fifteen-year-old prostitute because she hadn't been able to stop crying as he used her.

It had been a relief to get back to his office and turn his attention to other matters, but solving those matters was still a problem. Alec leaned back in his chair and looked at the sheets of paper spread out on the desk in front of him. Some sheets just had a few notes, others had several lines of his regular handwriting. Copies of the *Lucasville Trumpet* were set out too, the black typeface staring back at him. Alec had spent the last hour or so writing down his thoughts on Anderson, the Cornucopia Mine, the Northern Colorado Railroad,

Webb, the train robberies, Donegan and the articles in the *Trumpet*.

These things had to be connected somehow, but Alec couldn't quite put the pieces together to form a picture. Donegan and the silver had vanished. Had the outlaw now stolen enough to keep him quiet for a few months? Was he still in Dereham County? Alec absently rubbed his hand through his hair, ruffling it. He hadn't been able to find any personal reason for Anderson to attack Webb or his railroad, so why had Anderson bribed O'Connell to write those articles and then offered Alec money to ignore the dispute? What did Anderson stand to gain if the railroad went bust? Anderson needed that railroad to get his silver out of the mountains. Alec stared absently at the ceiling, trying to develop that thought. Anderson and the railroad needed one another. . . .

He was interrupted by a sharp knock on the door of his office. Alec blinked, then sat upright.

'Come in.'

The Lucasville marshal, Tom Clark, entered. Although he was only a few years older than Alec, his thick hair had already turned a shining steel-grey. No one would have mistaken him for an old man, though, as Tom Clark was firm-muscled and walked with the ease of an athlete. Alec greeted the marshal warmly, and shook his hand.

'It's a pleasure to see you, Tom,' Alec said, gathering the papers on his desk into a rough pile. 'What can I do for you?'

The marshal looked evenly across the desk at him,

his expression carefully controlled.

'I've come to give you some news, Alec, that you're sure as sin not going to like. Today I had to let Dench out on bail.'

'Dench? The son-of-a-bitch that was pestering Ei . . . Mrs Wessex?' Alec snapped.

Tom Clark nodded apologetically. 'I had no choice, Alec. His friends showed up with the bail money in cash and it was all legal.'

'Where did the likes of Finn and Buckton get five hundred dollars cash?' Alec demanded. 'It's no' pay-day, and even if it were, they wouldn't have that amount between them.'

'Finn said he'd had a lucky streak playing faro last night,' Clark explained. 'And other miners had clubbed in towards making up the difference.'

'I wouldna have thought a man like Dench would have so many friends,' Alec said sourly. He shook his head. 'Did Finn say where he got lucky?'

'At the Five Aces. I asked in there on the way here, and the manager confirmed it.'

The hot flush of Alec's temper had cooled, though the sense of frustration was still there. With the way things were going at the moment, there was a sense of inevitability about the marshal's news.

Alec sighed. 'So Dench is back on the streets to pester Eileen.'

Clark frowned. 'Mrs Wessex may not be the one he's most concerned with, don't forget. That's why I came to let you know he was out. He was always complaining that you'd got him locked up because you wanted Mrs

Wessex for yourself.' He shrugged slightly, indicating that he didn't believe Dench's allegations. 'He said he was going to make sure you couldn't interfere with "his" woman.'

'She's no' his!' Alec exclaimed, resisting the urge to thump his desk. 'She's a widow, she doesn't belong to any man; she's herself,' he finished, knowing what he meant but unable to express it clearly.

'That's not how Dench thinks,' the marshal warned. 'He thinks you're his rival and I'm certain sure he intends to do something about it.'

Alec took a couple of deep breaths, letting his temper cool, and began thinking.

'Thanks for coming to let me know,' he said, outwardly calmer. Glancing at the clock, he went on. 'I know ye didn't want to let him out, Tom, but we have to abide by the law and be seen to abide by the law. I'll not let Dench catch me unawares.'

'Good luck.'

They shook hands again, and the marshal departed, leaving Alec with new work to do.

When school finished for the day, Alec was waiting outside the hardware store on the opposite corner to the school building. It was the spot where Dench had waited for Eileen in the past. Alec's pose was casual, but his eyes were alert, searching for any sign of the miner amongst the people passing through the crossroads. There had been no sign of the miner by the time Eileen emerged from the schoolhouse. Alec couldn't help smiling at the sight of her. She was wearing a pale-green dress trimmed with cream lace, and the cream hat she'd had on the first time he'd met her. The effect was as fresh as the bright sky above, and Alec couldn't help contrasting her elegant appearance with Pearl Anderson's fussy ruffles and ribbons.

He crossed the street to join her, and was delighted to be welcomed by a smile.

'Sheriff Lawson,' she said warmly. 'It's nice to see you.'

Alec raised his hat to her. 'I'm pleased to see you too, Mrs Wessex. I just wish I was bringing better news to ye.'

Her eyes widened a little but she kept her composure. 'What is it?'

'I hafta tell ye that Dench was let out of jail this afternoon, on bail.'

'Oh.' This time Eileen couldn't keep the concern from her face. 'How did he raise the money!'

'Marshal Clark told me one of Dench's friends had a lucky streak at faro last night and put up the money,' Alec told her. 'I thought it best to come and see ye home safely.'

'Thank you,' Eileen said sincerely. She turned in the direction of her home and began walking, Alec alongside her. 'I do appreciate this,' she added, looking at him a little anxiously. 'But what will happen tomorrow and beyond? You and your deputies can't escort me everywhere I go.'

'I'm hoping that won't be necessary,' Alec answered decidedly.

As they walked, he continued to pay attention to their surroundings, glancing at doorways, the alleys between buildings and passers-by. Eileen let the subject drop.

'I hear you've been visiting with Mr Anderson recently,' she commented.

Alec turned his head to look at her, surprised. 'Where did ye hear that?'

She chuckled. 'Renee Winter and I both belong to the Lucasville Musical Society. She told me that she and her brother had been invited to dinner with the Andersons, and you had been too.'

Alec made a face. 'I should have remembered how fast news travels in a small town like Lucasville. You'd almost think they were using those telephone machines I've read about.'

'The speaking telegraph machines?' Eileen said. 'Yes, I've heard of them too. Isn't it wonderful, all these things that are being invented? It doesn't seem so long since the telegraph was the latest thing and now people can speak into a box and be heard miles away.'

'And all the gas lights people are having now,' Alec replied. 'Have ye seen the Tabor Grand Opera House in Denver? Gas lighting everywhere and the most beautiful chandelier in the auditorium. Very delicate it is, with crystals sparkling in the gaslight.'

'I've seen pictures but I've never seen it for real,' Eileen said, her eyes shining. 'You've been there?'

'I went with Karl to see *Othello,* and we both went back later with Sam and Ethan to see a minstrel show,' Alec confessed.

Eileen laughed delightfully. 'Shakespeare and minstrels; you have eclectic tastes, Sheriff.'

'I have eclectic friends,' he answered.

They continued to talk as they made their way through town towards Eileen's house. Alec was happy to be spending time with her, and with a good reason, but he couldn't afford to relax completely. If Eileen noticed his covert glances around at the buildings and wagons they passed, and the people on the streets, she pretended not to notice. So he wasn't entirely surprised when Dench jumped out from a narrow alley between buildings and launched himself into an attack.

Alec hadn't seen Dench armed before, but the flash of steel in the miner's hand gave him all the warning he needed. He wasn't sure if Dench was aiming for Eileen or himself, but bodily shoved the surprised woman out of the way. Dench lunged forward, shouting in anger, as he thrust his blade at Alec's chest.

Alec reacted without thinking, twisting aside and feeling the sting of the blade scraping across his ribs. For a moment, he was as close to sheer panic as he'd ever been, then the calm nerve that served him so well in combat took over. As Dench pulled back to attack again, Alec grabbed his knife arm and his shirt, pushing his leg between Dench's as he continued to swing around in the direction he'd turned. Dench tried to shift with him but caught his foot against Alec's leg and overbalanced. Alec didn't dare let go, but fell with him, landing mostly on top of Dench.

Dench barely seemed to notice, recovering far faster than Alec expected. He rolled over, throwing Alec off him and trapping Alec's right arm beneath his body. At the same time, he tried to bring the knife up to Alec's neck. Alec hung on grimly to Dench's wrist, exerting every ounce of strength to keep the blade from reaching his throat. The only sound was harsh gasps for breath as the two men wrestled for control of the blade.

The deadlock was broken by Alec. He brought his left knee up sharply, trying to hit Dench's groin. It wasn't a clean impact, but he hit hard enough to make Dench flinch. Alec seized the momentary advantage to push Dench's knife hand away from himself, and to roll away. He scrambled to his feet, as Dench did the same. Alec was barely off his knees when Dench swung the knife at him again. A frantic lurch backwards saved him. Catching his balance, Alec seized hold of Dench's knife hand as it passed in front of him. He pulled the arm further in the direction Dench had been striking, turning the other man round. Alec threw himself against Dench, using his weight to push him forward and into the wall of a nearby house.

Dench grunted, losing his breath briefly as Alec rammed him against the lumber planks. Alec slammed Dench's hand as hard as he could against the wall. The knife jolted from Dench's grasp and clattered to the floor. Bracing himself against the wall with his other hand, Dench shoved backwards hard. Alec staggered back, letting go of Dench's wrist in order to maintain his balance. Dench straightened up and whipped round in one move. A moment later, his hands closed on Alec's throat, cutting off his breath.

The strangling pressure jolted fear through Alec's body, but he didn't panic. He brought his arms up inside Dench's, then pushed outwards, hitting the inside of Dench's elbows so the joints buckled. Alec circled his arms out and down, pulling Dench's hands free from his neck. As Dench tried to lift his arms again, Alec jabbed a short punch into his nose. Dench cried out as he reeled back, giving Alec the chance to reach for his own knife.

'Surrender!' he yelled, bringing up the hunting knife in a fighting stance.

Dench caught his balance and lunged forward in a desperate move. As Alec slashed with his knife, Dench threw up his left arm to deflect the blade. Alec felt it slicing through the clothing and into the man's arm as Dench hurtled into him and knocked him backwards. Alec fell back on to the hard-packed dirt of the street again, the wind leaving him in an explosive grunt as Dench landed atop him, clinging to his clothing. He heard Eileen's cry of fear and anger, but didn't have time to think about her beyond the briefest sensation of being glad that she worried about him. The same cry served to spur Dench on in his anger.

'She's mine,' Dench hissed, his face a few inches from Alec's. 'You're dead.'

Alec sucked in a breath and stabbed with the knife in his right hand. As he'd guessed would happen, Dench grabbed his wrist. As Dench grabbed for the right wrist, Alec slammed the heel of his left hand into Dench's nose. Blood spattered out, splashing on to Alec's face, as the miner released his hold and reared backwards. Alec seized the advantage and threw Dench from him, rolling the other way. As he came to his knees, breathless and dishevelled, he heard an order snapped in Sam's familiar voice.

'Hold it, Dench. Surrender before I put daylight into you.'

Alec glanced first at Eileen as he scrambled to his feet. She looked worried but mighty relieved, and mustered a smile for him. Alec instinctively responded with a brief smile before turning his attention to Sam and Dench. Dench was lying on his back, both hands held in clear view, and a bitter expression on his face. Although Sam had both guns on him, Dench was staring at Alec.

'I'll fix you, Sheriff. I'll get loose and fix you good.'

Alec grunted, unimpressed, and looked at Sam. He had arranged for his deputy to follow, keeping out of sight, as his backup, when he'd decided to draw Dench out by using himself as bait.

'What took you so long?' Alec demanded.

Sam's eyes darted towards Eileen and sparked with humour. ''You seemed to be handling things pretty darn well on your lonesome,' he replied. 'I figgered as you didn't need much help from me.'

Alec felt himself colour slightly, but couldn't think of anything suitable to say in Eileen's presence. He settled for scowling at Dench instead.

'I've got witnesses that say ye threatened me, and two witnesses to show you attacked me. Your friends aren't going to be able to afford bail this time. You're staying behind bars and serving a long sentence,' he told Dench, putting away the hunting knife.

When Dench had been searched and cuffed, Sam offered to take him to the marshal's office.

'You sure could do with getting yourself fixed up some, boss,' he said, keeping one gun pointed at Dench in a deceptively casual manner.

'He's right,' Eileen agreed. 'My house is just along here and you can get cleaned up there.'

Alec agreed, and as Sam pushed the sullen Dench away, he followed Eileen in the opposite direction.

Eileen Wessex's house was a pleasant lumber building, surrounded by a picket fence that enclosed the beginnings of a flower garden. Alec followed her inside and into the parlour. He sat where she indicated, in a comfortable, leather-upholstered armchair. She looked at him, anxious again.

'Take your jacket off and sit comfortable while I get some warm water and a cloth.' She glanced at the patch of blood soaking into his shirt where Dench's knife had scraped across his ribs. 'That certainly needs attention.'

Alec was on the point of protesting that he could go to the doctor, but the urge to be fussed over by Eileen kept him silent as she bustled away into the kitchen. Alec removed his brown jacket, leaned back in his chair, and relaxed, for what seemed like the first time in days. His side hurt, he was dirty, and he knew he'd have bruises from the rough and tumble, but he was satisfied. He'd spoken to Tom Clark, the town marshal, before setting off to lure out Dench, and knew that the marshal would keep Dench behind bars until his trial.

Eileen's house was welcoming, and Alec preferred it to the Andersons' fussy parlour and dining room. There were plenty of books, neatly shelved, a small upright piano with an embroidered stool and a vase of dainty white wildflowers on the table that Alec recognized as northern bedstraw. It was far more homelike than the haphazardly furnished and mostly functional rooms of the living quarters he shared with his deputies. He looked about with interest, for a few minutes losing himself in the fantasy of living here, with Eileen as his wife.

She reappeared after a few minutes, carrying a wooden box in one hand, a cloth-covered bowl in the other, and with a white shirt draped over one shoulder. Eileen put the box and bowl on a small table close to Alec's chair and lay the shirt over the arm of a rocking chair near the fireplace. She studied him for a moment before speaking.

'If you sit forward and take off your vest and shirt I'll see to that knife wound on your side first.'

'My shirt?' Alec protested. 'I don't—'

She smiled at him. 'I've been married, so it's quite appropriate for me to tend you. And I've fixed up wounds before, so I know what I'm doing.'

'I . . . er . . . guess so,' Alec answered. Mercifully, she turned away as he stripped off neckerchief, vest and shirt to reveal his graceful, slender-waisted torso.

Eileen took the blood-stained clothing from him.

'I'll wash and mend these before I return them,' she said. 'And before you protest that you can send them to the laundry, this is my thanks for what you've done in listening to me, and getting Dench put behind bars. Not many men would have done the same.'

'Any of my deputies would have,' Alec protested anyway.

Eileen smiled. 'Yes, *your* deputies would have. But you set the example by taking the risks. Now sit right forward so I can see that knife wound.'

Alec gave up the argument and obeyed.

Eileen washed him gently with the cloth wrung out in warm water, which smelt of some patent disinfectant. It stung when she wiped the drying blood away from the shallow cut over his ribs, but Alec gritted his teeth and stayed still. When she was satisfied, Eileen opened the wooden box and extracted one of the small bottles from inside. This she shook vigorously before pouring a little of the contents on a scrap of cotton wool, that she stroked carefully around the wound.

'This will help to numb it,' she explained, taking up a needle and thread. 'It will be better for a few stitches.'

'All right,' Alec consented, turning his head to stare at bookshelves.

The local anaesthetic helped, but he was still clenching his teeth and curling his hands into fists as Eileen stitched quickly and neatly. When she was done, he let out a long sigh, and relaxed as she bandaged him, and daubed witch hazel on the bruises that were beginning to show.

'Put that on and I'll clean your face,' Eileen instructed, handing him the shirt.

As Alec had suspected, it was too large for him, but at least he could adjust the sleeve length with the sleeve suspenders he'd been wearing on his own shirt. He sat back into the chair and closed his eyes at Eileen dabbed away the dirt and blood he'd accumulated during the fight. Alec couldn't see her, but he could hear the rustle of her dress as she moved, smell the clean scent of her hands and relish the gentle touch of those hands against his face. This time he was sorry when she was done.

'Now you rest, and I'll fetch coffee,' she promised, gathering up her things and packing items neatly back into the boxes.

Alec felt himself reviving as he sipped the good coffee, and felt up to more conversation.

'How are ye doing here in Lucasville?' he asked Eileen, who was sitting on another chair, also with a cup of coffee.

'I'm really feeling quite at home,' she told him. 'The schoolwork is satisfying and it's good to have a purpose. I'd feel so useless, just sitting here in the house on my own.'

'What about the music?' Alec asked, indicating the piano. 'That must be a source of pleasure for ye, and company, being a member of the town Musical Society.'

'It is,' she answered, smiling. 'Music does make my life richer.' She paused, and looked nostalgic in a way that touched Alec's heart. 'I just wish I could hear it in the proper surroundings again, like a lovely opera house with a full, professional orchestra.'

'I would like' – Alec started, intending to ask her to accompany him to a concert at the Tabor Opera House. He saw her eyes widen, and suddenly remembered that she had been widowed a year ago, and that he was wearing her dead husband's shirt – 'to hear a concert myself, someday,' he finished awkwardly.

Eileen's expression stayed still and incomprehensible. 'I'm sure you will have the chance, Sheriff,' she answered in flat tones.

Alec wanted to kick himself for offending her. Instead, he carefully set down the coffee cup and slowly stood up.

'Ye've done a fine job of fixing me up,' he said, keeping his voice neutral. 'I'm very grateful to ye, Mrs Wessex, but I'd best be getting back to my office now.'

Eileen stood up too, and gracefully offered him her hand. 'I can't express my thanks at how you've helped me,' she said formally. 'I'll return your shirt and vest in a couple of days.'

'Thank you, and thank you for the loan of this shirt,' he replied, taking her hand for a brief grasp, and resisting his wish to hold on to it for longer. Her large brown eyes seemed to search his face for a few moments, then she looked down. They exchanged goodbyes and Alec left, sore where the knife had scored across his ribs, and unaccountably sore in his heart.

CHAPTER ELEVEN

The next day, Alec threw himself into his work, tackling the paperwork that he'd been putting off. By mid morning, he was feeling more sociable, and ready to leave his office and join the others in the central office, where the new copy of the *Lucasville Trumpet* was being shared out.

Ethan stared mournfully at the back of the section of paper that he held. 'Story continued on page 10,' he read aloud, and examined his pages closely. 'Who's got page 10?'

Sam immediately denied having the necessary page, as did Karl, once he'd handed a few of his sheets to Alec.

'Someone must have it,' Ethan declared. 'Unless they done printed the paper with pages missing,' he added with practised melancholy.

Alec scanned the first page he'd been given. 'It's here.' He started to hold out the section of newspaper, then withdrew it from Ethan's fingers to look at it more closely.

'The story won't make sense unless you've read the first part,' Ethan pleaded, holding out his own section of newspaper.

Alec shook his head. 'There's an advertisement here, from the Northern Colorado Railroad Company.'

'That's Webb's company,' Karl remarked.

'Webb's selling shares in his railroad,' Alec said, studying the page thoughtfully. His deputies fell silent, watching their leader.

'Webb told us that investors had been put off by the newspaper articles; that they were selling their shares, and the shares were getting less valuable all the time. Those newspaper articles have driven down the price of the shares.' He looked around at the others. 'We ken how Anderson paid for those newspaper articles. Eil . . . Mrs Wessex saw him leaving the newspaper office and the editor confirmed it to me. I thought maybe Anderson wanted to drive Webb out of business but couldna think why he'd want to do that when he needs the railroad to move his silver.

'I got my thinking backwards. Anderson doesn't want to close down the railroad; he wants to *buy shares* in the railroad, so he doesn't have to pay someone else to ship his silver, and he makes money from everyone else using the railroad. He's gonna get those shares at rock-bottom prices.' His face suddenly lit up. 'We never found out where his silver went – what Donegan was going to do with all that bullion. I bet that bullion's back at Anderson's mine, waiting to be shipped out again, and Donegan's got some cash money instead, to spend as his payment.'

131

'You know, boss, that's a swell plan,' Sam drawled in admiration.

'It sounds plausible,' Karl agreed. 'But how are we going to show that Anderson's the guilty party?'

Alec began to pace back and forth as his quick mind thought up plans.

'We need to show that Anderson and Donegan are linked. If we pass some information to Anderson, and Donegan acts on it, I'll know I'm right. We need to find a way of getting Donegan into the open.'

'I'm sure you'll do it,' Karl said with quiet confidence.

'Can I have my section of the paper now,' Ethan pleaded.

'What will you do if Anderson doesn't take your bait?' Ethan asked Alec Lawson.

They were sitting on a bench built against the wall of a caboose, as the train wound through the valleys, following the South St Vrain River towards Lucasville.

'Look a fool,' Alec answered, swaying as the train slowed for a corner.

They were riding at the rear of a specially commissioned train, supposedly carrying bullion down from the mines to Lucasville. The locomotive was drawing four boxcars, allegedly carrying bullion and a few other goods from the mining district, and the caboose. Alec had 'let slip' to Anderson that this trip was a make-or-break for the Northern Colorado; if it were to be robbed, the railroad would go bust. Alec had never in his life longed for a train to be held up, but he did so now.

He stood up, moving easily through the gently swaying caboose to the raised chair provided for the guard to sit and look out through the raised cupola that sat mid-way along the roof. A guard would sit there and look out, watching along his train for problems, while sheltered from the weather.

'If they're gonna jump us, where do you reckon it will be?' Ethan asked, his expression suggesting that no such event would happen.

'There's a couple of places, but my best guess would be around Deadman Gulch.'

'It would be,' Ethan replied with studied gloom.

Alec grinned. 'I thought you'd like that.' He took hold of the chair and nimbly climbed up to peer out. 'I reckon we're not far off,' he called, looking at the scenery as it rolled past.

He scrambled down again and went to peer cautiously through the left window on the caboose.

'You had to ride in here, and you know it,' Ethan said, with more sympathy than before.

Alec knew what he meant. The robbers would most likely concentrate on the boxcars with the sealed boxes supposedly containing bullion. Alec would have preferred to be there himself, but after confronting Donegan in the saloon shoot-out at Caribou, there was too great a chance that Ethan or himself would be recognized immediately. Sam had been present at the first train robbery, but Alec hoped the thieves hadn't seen him properly. So Karl and Sam were in one of the boxcars, and Alec was at the rear of the train with

Ethan. The engineer and fireman were employees of the railroad, and the four lawmen were the only other men aboard.

The train left the narrow canyon and wound its way along a spectacular valley with a wider floor. Trees bursting with the green of early summer hung from the rocky slopes, and Alec caught a glimpse of a lacy, white waterfall tumbling down the mountainside as the train rattled past. For a moment, he was thinking how much he would like to drive out here in a buggy, and show this landscape to Eileen. Then the locomotive's whistle sounded, and he lifted his head like a hunter sensing prey.

There was another whistle, and the cars began to clatter together as the train slowed. Alec peered out of the window in the door at the front of the carriage, grimacing as the cars bumped one another. He had heard of air brakes being used back East, which were operated by the engineer and would control all the cars at once. Out here, each car was slowed individually, by a brakeman who climbed to the roof of each car in turn in order to operate the brakewheels set there. There was no brakeman on this train, however, and the only brake being used now was on the locomotive. The train slowed unevenly, cars crashing together, and Alec and Ethan both found themselves holding on to the fittings to brace themselves until the train was at rest.

The locomotive hissed as it let off steam. Both men kept their hands on the butts of their guns as they listened as best they could to voices up ahead. They heard shouting, and the distinctive sound of a boxcar door rumbling open. Ethan closed up behind Alec as he listened at the door at the front, and peered cautiously through the window. Alec quietly unfastened the door and pulled it open, leaving them free to step on to the tiny, railed platform at the front of the caboose.

With a boost from Ethan, Alec reached over the rails to the iron ladder on the rear of the boxcar in front, and began climbing. He was most of the way up when the train jerked and began moving again. Alec clung tightly to the ladder as the train gathered speed once again. He glanced back at Ethan, who looked at him questioningly.

'They must be moving the train to rendezvous with the pack horses,' Alec suggested, as quietly as he could given the noise of the train. 'Maybe they thought we had someone in the hills expecting them to stop the train just here.'

Ethan nodded, and gestured for Alec to keep climbing.

Alec did so, peering cautiously over the top of the boxcar as the wind whipped at his hat. He saw two of the outlaws sitting on top of the boxcar ahead, where Karl and Sam were. He recognized the black man, Henley, that Liston had wounded during the first robbery, and a balding man named Shotton. Neither were yet looking his way, but were watching opposite sides of the canyon with rifles in hand, which supported his theory that they were expecting an ambush themselves. Carefully, Alec wriggled on top of the box car, drew his revolver, and began crawling. Faint noises from behind told him that Ethan was doing the same.

He was about halfway along the roof of the boxcar, when he heard shots from the car where Karl and Sam were. He was scared for them, but knew that the only way he could help now was to deal with the two outlaws on the roof. They both looked down first, then towards one another. As they turned, Henley spotted the two lawmen on the roof of the car behind.

'Look out!' he yelled, raising his rifle.

Alec dropped flat, feeling the tug of Eileen's stitches in his barely healed side, taking a fast shot as he fell. The shot missed Henley, but distracted him enough that the outlaw's own shot went wild. Behind and to one side, Ethan opened up too. The outlaws were sitting, and were the larger targets. Alec had no time to demand a surrender: only to shoot. Shotton returned Ethan's fire, the shot slapping between the lawmen. Alec got his next shot off before Henley, and saw the outlaw rock as the bullet ripped though his upper arm. Henley pulled his rifle's trigger reflexively, but his shot went skywards. As Alec fired, Ethan and Shotton exchanged near misses again. Alec changed his aim and fired at Shotton too. The outlaw tumbled backwards, hit by both lawmen, and dropped his rifle. Alec instantly switched his attention back to the wounded Henley.

'Throw down the rifle!'

Henley had been trying to raise the rifle to shoulder height, mostly using his left hand. He gave up, tossing the rifle towards the lawmen.

'Don't shoot,' he yelled back, the wind tugging at his

136

hat. 'I'm hurt.'

While Ethan continued to cover him, Alec sat up and slid more shells into his revolver. Only then did he rise to his feet and walk carefully along the top of the fast-moving boxcar, making the three-foot jump to the next.

'Throw your knife and pistol over the side,' Alec ordered.

Henley obeyed awkwardly, his right arm now limp at his side as blood soaked through the torn shirtsleeve. As Ethan moved up behind them, Alec spared a quick glance at Shotton. The balding man lay still, two holes in his chest and his eyes open and filming over.

'Where's Donegan?' Alec demanded.

Henley gave a sullen stare before answering. 'He's in the engine cab.'

Alec nodded acknowledgement. He moved to the edge of the boxcar, lay down, and peered over the edge. The door below was open, so he swung down over the edge, clinging to the handholds there and ignoring the pain in his side. Cautiously, he peered around the doorway, and found himself staring into the muzzle of an Army Colt.

'Good,' said Karl, lowering the Colt. 'It's you. Come on in.'

He helped Alec swing himself in through the doorway. Inside, it seemed dark after the bright sunshine outside, and it took a few moments for Alec's eyes to adjust. Looking about, he saw a red-haired outlaw lying sprawled on the floor, a bullet hole in the centre of his forehead. An outlaw that Alec recognized as someone called Halliwell, and a scruffy individual with a surly expression, called Formby, were sitting on the floor, handcuffed. Sam was at the back of the car, winding a black bandanna around his right thigh. As he was wearing his own, gaudy bandanna, Alec correctly guessed that the black one had come from one of the outlaws.

Sam looked up at Alec and grinned, looking roguish, rather than hurt.

'It's messy, not bad,' he said. 'Still, got that one plumb between the eyes, for sure.'

'You two are staying here then,' Alec ordered. 'Ethan and I'll take on Donegan.'

'Just be careful,' Karl said.

Alec gave him a reckless grin. 'As ever,' he promised.

Karl gave him a hand on to the handholds, and he was soon back on top of the boxcar as the train rumbled onwards.

Ethan greeted him with a typical remark.

'I reckon Donegan knows he's got company.'

'Then we'd best go join him,' Alec answered.

'What about me?' Henley whimpered, clutching at his bleeding arm. Shock had started to set in, and his face was white beneath its tan.

'You can make yourself a bandage from your bandanna,' Alec told him. 'And hope that someone gets back to you before you faint and roll off this boxcar.'

Ignoring Henley's moan of distress, he led Ethan forwards along the train.

They had left Deadman Gulch now, and were in a narrow, steep-sided valley. The train ran along an embankment that gave way to a rocky path carved out of the side of the cliff, high above the valley floor, as they approached the first of two sharp corners. Alec had no time to admire the spectacular scenery; he knew that they needed to get Donegan out of the locomotive cab as soon as possible. This thought gave him all the motivation he needed to make the jump from one gently swaying boxcar to the next as the train sped along, gradually gaining speed as it moved down the gradient.

Ethan was alongside him, his long face taut, but he made no complaints about the dangers they were risking as they made their way forward. A brisk breeze tugged at hats and clothes as they moved atop the boxcars, smoke from the locomotive ahead puffing past in strings. With the increasing drop to the right, they seemed an awful long way off the ground, as the train moved beneath them. As they jogged cautiously along the roof of the car, they heard a shot from the direction of the locomotive. Alec swore under his breath. Moments later, he glimpsed a figure in overalls falling off the train from up ahead. The limp figure tumbled outwards, rolling to the edge of the embankment as the train sped past.

'Damn Donegan. That was the engineer.'

Ethan paused to peer over the right side of the car.

'Fireman's gone too; I reckon he's jumped.'

Alec picked up his pace, leaping without thought across the gap to the roof of the car behind the tender. He had his gun in his hand now, as did Ethan.

They were halfway along when Donegan's head

139

popped up from behind the far end of the timber-filled tender. The outlaw's face, with blue eyes in his tanned, part-Indian face, was distinctive; Henley had been telling the truth. Alec flung himself on to his belly, triggering a quick shot as he did so. He missed, but the shot was enough to distract Donegan's aim. Moments later, he heard Ethan hit the wooden roof too, landing with a breathless grunt. Alec fired again, but Donegan had already ducked behind the cover of the tender, only to pop up a moment later in another place, and send a shot over Alec's head. Ethan took a potshot and missed as the outlaw ducked again. Alec rolled over, ending up closer to the edge than he would have wished, but not where Donegan's next shot went. Both lawmen fired, but their poor position, the moving train and Donegan's cover made him hard to hit. By this time, the sharp right-hand turn was looming up ahead. Alec crabbed to his left, gritting his teeth against the stab of the knife wound from Dench, and getting even closer to the edge. When Donegan popped up again, he'd clearly expected the lawman to take the safer option of moving inwards, as his shot went down the centre of the boxcar. Alec's shot missed, but Ethan's came close enough to make the outlaw duck back more hurriedly than before.

At this moment, the train reached the sharp turn at Little Narrows.

'Hang on,' Alec yelled to Ethan, flattening himself against the roof of the boxcar.

The train swerved abruptly to the right, throwing both men sideways. Alec found himself sliding closer to the edge of the roof. He frantically dug fingers and boot-toes into the gaps between the planks the car was built from. As the car took the corner, it swayed over so far the right wheels left the track completely. Alec's left leg swung over into empty space, his foot scant inches from the solid rock of the fast-passing canyon wall. Ethan glanced across at him, his face white with fear. He was clinging on hard himself, and was too far away to risk letting go and making a grab for his friend. Alec gritted his teeth against the pain surging in his side, mentally cursing Dench and his jealousy. As the pain grew worse, Alec had no choice but to release his revolver and watch it slide away until hitting the shallow lip of the roof. With his right hand now free, Alec could grip the cracks in the roof more firmly, and give himself a better chance of surviving.

CHAPTER TWELVE

With his heart pounding and his fingers aching from their death-grip, Alec hung on until the careering train rounded the corner and their boxcar settled back on to all its wheels. Breathless from exertion and pain, he hauled himself fully back on to the roof and snatched up his gun with his left hand.

Fortunately, Donegan must have been clinging on himself during the wild manoeuvre, as he didn't pop up to take advantage of the lawmen's misfortune. This time, instead of changing position, Alec chose to stay where he was, and brace his pistol with both hands.

'Herd him to me,' he instructed.

'Got you, boss,'

When Donegan popped up again, he'd expected the lawman to move to the centre of the boxcar. Instead, his intended target was still on the edge of the flat roof Again, Donegan's bullet passed harmlessly between the two lawmen. Ethan took the first shot in return, aiming just to the outlaw's left, causing him to reflexively jerk right. He moved directly into Alec's aim, and took his bullet in the head. Donegan's head snapped backwards with the impact, and he fell out of sight.

Alec didn't wait, but scrambled to his feet and hurried forwards. He jumped down into the tender, landing among the logs on his knees and free hand. He gasped at the jab of pain in his side, but picked himself up, and climbed over the wood, Ethan faithfully behind him. When he reached the end, gun at the ready, he found his precaution was unnecessary. Donegan was sprawled across the floor of the cab, a neat hole in his forehead. Holstering his gun, Alec scrambled down into the cab, hard-pressed not to tread on the body.

'Stay up there,' he called to Ethan. 'I need ye to start turning the brakewheels.'

'Right.' Ethan turned and looked at the boxcars behind them. 'Boss, I think there's a bigger gap between the second and third cars.'

'Godammit!' Alec said fiercely. 'She's broke in two. Brake the second car halfway, and try to alert Karl. You're *not* to try jumping the gap at any cost, hear me? Then brake halfway on the first boxcar, back to the second, and wait for my signal to brake fully. Got that.'

'Yes, sir,' Ethan barked, and turned to scramble away.

Alec climbed fully into the cabin of the locomotive, and scanned the array of controls in front him, silently praying that he could slow the train safely.

His only experience of actually driving a locomotive had been picking one up from where the engineer had left her and moving her into the roundhouse. He'd never controlled a full train, let alone one at speed. The first thing he recognized was the long handle of the regulator and he promptly threw this over to cut the speed. Looking to the left, Alec found the screw reverser. He twisted it anticlockwise, switching steam to the opposite end of the pistons, reversing the direction of the wheels. The engine lurched and stuttered and from behind came the crash and shove of the remaining cars piling unevenly into one another.

Alec hoped frantically that Ethan was still aboard, but didn't have time to turn and look for him. And if Ethan had fallen, there was nothing Alec could do for him anyway. Reaching up, he took two sharp tugs on the whistle, signalling for the boxcar brakes to be applied fully. There was another shunt from behind, possibly the now separate rear section piling into the gradually slowing front half. Alec took a moment to glance through one of the cab windows. Up ahead, the track followed the curve of the canyon wall, turning sharply to the left. The train would heel over to its right, with nothing between it and the sheer drop to the canyon floor maybe a hundred feet below.

There was only one thing left for Alec to do. He hauled on the brake lever, the blocks squealing as they pressed against the massive wheels. The whole train shuddered as boxcars piled against one another. Alec clung to the controls as the corner came rushing ever closer. The train was slowing, but he had no idea whether it was slowing sufficiently to make the curve. Heart beating hard, he assessed his options. If he tried to jump out to the left, he would be jumping into the rocky canyon wall, barely three feet away. If the impact of that didn't kill him, chances were high that he'd

144

bounce off it and end up falling under the moving train. To his right was just a couple of feet of the rocky path carved from the side of the canyon for the track. Beyond was a long drop down the side of the canyon, through trees and rocks, to the canyon floor. Gritting his teeth, and sending silent prayers for the lives of his friends, Alec hung on for dear life.

The rattling, juddering locomotive, wheels squealing, swept into the corner. As it heeled to the right, Alec instinctively moved to the left of the cabin, though his weight could make no difference in counterbalancing that of the locomotive. Donegan's body slid across the floor of the cabin, and Alec suddenly wondered how the injured Henley was managing on the roof of a boxcar. More importantly, he hoped that Ethan was hanging on, as the train teetered around the curve. Alec held his breath until he felt light-headed. Somehow, miraculously, the slowing train clung to the rails and turned into the wider valley.

Alec let out his breath in a sudden rush and sucked in another deep one. Releasing his white-knuckled grip, he turned and climbed up the tender to look at the rest of the train. His heart gave a huge bound in his chest as he saw the raised cupola of the caboose still at the rear of the train. Every car had made it, and even better, he saw Ethan clinging to a brakewheel, his arms locked about it. Alec leapt back into the cab, noticing that the train was really starting to lose speed now. Exultantly, he pulled on the whistle, relieving his feelings with a series of triumphant blasts.

*

145

The train eventually stopped partway along a wooden trestle that took the tracks from the canyon-side to a spur of high ground that ran part way across the canyon floor. Alec jumped down from the cabin and jogged back along the trestle, ignoring the painful stitches in his side. Ethan crawled to the edge of his boxcar roof and looked down at him.

'That's the last time I ever get on a train with you, Alec.'

Alec grinned up at him. 'You walking back to Lucasville then?'

Ethan scowled, and began climbing down.

Alec made his way to the boxcar his other friends were in. Karl had appeared at the doorway, apparently as composed as ever. 'You know, I'm glad we couldn't see those corners coming from inside our car.' He looked at Alec thoughtfully. 'You must have had a grand view from the locomotive cab,' he said, apparently casually.

Alec nodded. 'I sure did,' he replied quietly. 'I don't know what would be worse: seeing the curves coming, or not knowing.'

'Well, we didn't lose anyone from inside,' Karl said philosophically.

Alec looked over at Ethan. 'Is Henley still up top?' he asked.

Ethan nodded. 'Don't know if he's done fainted or died, but he's still up there, bundled up alongside of Shotton.'

'We'd best bring them down,' Alec decided. 'The dead ones can travel in their own car. We'd best fix that

146

break, and reverse back to look for the engineer and the fireman.'

Alec and Sam jury-rigged a fix for the broken coupling, while Ethan and Karl brought Henley down from the roof of the boxcar, and laid him beside the handcuffed Halliwell and Formby. The bodies were moved to another boxcar and covered with sacks. When they were ready, Karl accompanied Alec back to the locomotive cab to act as temporary fireman. Ethan climbed up top again to release the brakewheels. After checking that the screw reverser was still on full reverse, Alec took a deep breath, opened the regulator, and released the engine brakes. Slowly, the locomotive began to steam backwards, pushing the boxcars back up the gradient towards the double curves.

Alec was too cautious at first, the engine making little headway against the weight behind it. Cautiously, he opened the regulator further, but even so, there was no danger in the speed at which he took the curves. The ride was uneven, many of the wheels along the train having flat-spotted under the intense braking, but Alec frankly didn't care. His hunch about Anderson's involvement in the robberies had been proven, and more importantly, he was bringing his friends out alive.

The train eventually reached the section of embankment where they found the engineer's body, shot by Donegan, and the fireman. Ethan's guess had been right: the fireman had jumped, after seeing his engineer get shot in cold blood. He had survived with a broken leg and multiple contusions. He was loaded aboard, and insisted on giving a myriad of instructions to Karl, indignant at having to let someone else take his place in his precious cab. At last, they set off back to Lucasville.

It was almost noon by the time Alec drove the train back to the station in town. He spoke briefly to Webb, who came hurrying out from his office to greet them. The stocky railroad owner made a brief comment about the state of the damaged wheels, but his overall relief was evident as Alec reassured him that he had evidence enough to arrest Anderson. Webb unbent long enough to deal Alec a hearty thump on the shoulder by way of thanks.

'You done real good, Sheriff,' he growled.

The surviving outlaws were taken to the county jail, where Alec questioned them. He didn't get many answers from the surly Formby, but the oldest gang member, Halliwell, was more usefully forthcoming. Alec left Ethan filling in paperwork while Sam had his wounded leg fixed up by a doctor. Taking Karl with him, Alec stopped back at the sheriff's office, before mounting up, and riding out to the Cornucopia Mine.

Alec sat comfortably in the deep saddle, relaxing as Biscuit jogged along the trail. He reached forward and affectionately rubbed his knuckles on the horse's firm, tawny neck.

'Give me a real horse over an iron horse every day,' he remarked.

'You handled the iron horse well enough,' said Karl, sitting well on his own dark-chestnut gelding.

Alec suppressed a shudder at the memory of the locomotive veering around the curves, so close to disaster. 'I wouldna do that again if you paid me a thousand dollars.'

'It's over and we all came out alive,' Karl reminded him. 'And now we're going to arrest the man responsible.'

Alec nodded. 'Aye, that's right.' He pushed the memory to the back of his mind, and switched his attention to the beautiful scenery they were riding through, as they headed upriver again, this time to Stone Canyon.

They heard the mine before they saw it, the thudding of the stamp mills carrying though the crisp mountain air. Alec shook his head, wondering how anyone could stand to work amid such noise. The pounding brought him sharply back to the present, setting his mind on the task ahead of him. They followed the well-worn trail that led to the mine, slowing the horses to a walk to let them cool off. When they came within sight of the mine buildings, set in a large clearing cut into the forest, the two lawmen split up. Alec rode straight to the main office buildings, while Karl circled around, keeping out of sight.

Alec dismounted outside the main office, patting his horse and loosening the girths a little to let it rest more comfortably. Leaving it tied to a hitching rail, he pushed open the door and let himself into the cool dimness of the front office.

'Good afternoon, er . . . Sheriff.' The thin clerk there hurriedly put down his pen. 'Can we help you?'

'I want to see Mr Anderson,' Alec replied confidently.

'Uh, certainly.' The clerk bobbed a small bow as he stood up. Alec remembered this behaviour from a previous visit, knowing it meant nothing more than habitual nervousness on the man's behalf.

The thin clerk knocked timidly on Anderson's office door, and opened it just far enough to put his head around and speak to his boss. Alec automatically checked the set of his pistol in its holster, and checked the inside pocket of his comfortable brown jacket. He was already moving when the clerk turned to beckon him in.

'Mr Anderson can see you right away, sir,' he sputtered.

'Thank you,' Alec said graciously, pushing the office door fully open to let himself in, before closing it again. The room was as he remembered it from a previous visit, well furnished, as became a successful businessman, without being ostentatious in its fittings. Anderson's hat hung from a curly coat-stand beside the door, and a fancy lamp sat unlit on the corner of the walnut desk. The sash window was open a few inches, allowing a gentle breeze to freshen the air and billow the lace curtains.

Anderson rose to his feet behind his desk, offering one of his broad hands for Alec to shake. He smiled, revealing the square, prominent teeth that helped give him the look of a draught animal.

'I hope your presence means good news, Sheriff Lawson,' he said, repeating himself with 'Good news,' again.

'I reckon it does,' Alec replied, taking a seat as Anderson sat down again with his desk between them. 'Not such good news for Donegan, I'm afraid.'

Anderson's pale brown eyes widened anxiously. 'Do tell, Sheriff, do tell.'

'Well, Donegan somehow got word about the special train, and tried to rob it. What he didna get told was that myself and my deputies were aboard that train.' Alec paused briefly, watching the panic flash up in Anderson's eyes. 'You see, I had an inkling that he might make a try for the bullion, so I was waiting for him,' Alec went on.

'Is Donegan dead?' Anderson asked urgently, leaning forward across his desk.

Alec nodded. 'I shot him myself and I don't regret it for a minute,' he added honestly.

Relief and anxiety both flickered on Anderson's long face, as he regarded Alec with deeper respect than the sheriff had seen from him before.

'Of course,' Alec went on smoothly. 'We didna kill all his men. Took three of them alive, in fact.'

'Three? Where are they now?' Anderson asked.

'Down at the county jail,' Alec told him. 'And very helpful they've been too. Only too pleased to sign confessions saying what happened to the Cornucopia's bullion that they took from the earlier robberies.'

Anderson went white. 'You surely don't believe everything those outlaws and ruffians have to say; those outlaws.'

Alec smiled coolly. 'As it happens, I do believe them. You see, there's no way Donegan should ha' known about the train this morning. It wasn't a regular schedule; it was put on only yesterday. No one was told about it, and what was supposed to be on it. I just happened to let slip the details to you, and you passed them on to Donegan.'

CHAPTER THIRTEEN

'You can't prove that,' Anderson replied, clinging to his dignity.

'The confessions of Donegan's men prove it,' Alec answered. 'You tried to drive down the share prices of the railroad so ye could buy them up cheaply yourself.'

'I'm a miner, a mine owner, not a railroad man,' Anderson protested.

'And ye need that railroad to transport mine goods and the bullion,' Alec countered. He leaned back in his chair, suddenly seeming relaxed. 'Of course, you haven't killed anyone yourself. I might be willing to . . . overlook . . . your part in all this.'

In spite of his outwardly calm demeanour, Alec's heart was pounding. Bringing up the topic of the bribe that he believed Anderson had offered earlier was one of the hardest things he'd ever done. He forced himself to appear relaxed as he waited for Anderson's response.

Anderson stared across the desk at him for a silent minute, then the man's face cleared.

'I'm not quite sure what you mean, Sheriff,' he said cautiously.

Alec tilted his head slightly to one side. 'Well, somebody sent me seven hundred dollars in cash, with a note asking me to mind my own business over the matter of the Northern Colorado Railroad.'

Anderson took a deep breath, running a large hand over his carefully arranged, pomaded hair. 'Seven hundred dollars is a lot of money, a lot of money.'

'Aye,' Alec agreed, keeping his calm appearance while waiting for Anderson to make the next move.

Anderson picked up his pen and fiddled with it. 'It's a lot of money.'

'The sort of money a man could put to good use,' Alec answered. 'But not much compared to what owning the majority share in a railroad would be worth.'

Anderson took in a deep breath. 'I could double it, double it.' His knuckles were white as he clenched the pen in his hand.

'Double it?' Alec queried, fighting to remain calm himself. He shook his head. 'You hired Donegan and he killed two good men. He nearly got more killed this morning. You've committed fraud and abetted a robber, Mr Anderson.'

Anderson raised his head, and looked straight across the desk. 'I'll give you two thousand dollars to forget what you know about my involvement in this,' he said, his voice trembling.

Alec simply stared back at him, his contempt clear in his eyes.

'Two thousand dollars doesn't buy the lives of the men who died because of your greed,' he answered. 'Twenty thousand wouldn't buy me off.'

He reached into the inner pocket of his jacket and withdrew a paper. 'I'm arresting you on charges of fraud, deception, conspiracy and attempted bribery of a law enforcement officer.'

Anderson swallowed, and tried to fight back. 'You can't prove I tried to bribe you.'

Alec raised his voice slightly. 'Did you hear it, Karl?'

Karl Firth appeared on the outside of the open office window, looking at Anderson with a contempt equal to Alec's.

'He just offered you two thousand dollars,' Karl said clearly.

Anderson's face fell, and he slumped back into his chair. He emitted a sob, then burst out. 'Pearl doesn't know about it. She doesn't know anything about Donegan, not Donegan.'

Alec grunted. 'You're the one who will be standing trial. A wife canna be witness against her husband.'

'Don't put her on trial,' Anderson pleaded. 'She's a good woman.'

'Then she probably deserved better than you,' Alec answered, standing up and taking a set of handcuffs from his pocket.

Anderson sagged, any remaining fight leaving him as Alec approached and applied the cuffs.

'Come on.' Alec gave him a gentle push towards the door. 'Back to town. You've got an appointment at the jail.'

Anderson's arrest was a bonus for O'Connell, the editor of the *Lucasville Trumpet*, if for no one else. The paper's circulation soared with the stories of Anderson's wrongdoing, and Sheriff Alec Lawson found himself hailed as a hero, much to the amusement of his deputies. He put up with the teasing, only too relieved to know they were all safe and well after the terrifying train ride that he relived in his dreams. Sam was still limping from his leg wound, but it was healing well. Eileen's stitches had held together under the strains of the fight on the moving train, and Alec almost forgot about his injury.

He couldn't forget entirely, not least because he was the main witness at Dench's trial for assault, which took place just a couple of days later. At Alec's request, the prosecution was arranged so that Eileen Wessex didn't need to appear in the courthouse. With the threats that Dench had made in front of his friends, and the attacks on Alec that Karl and Sam had witnessed, there was plenty of evidence to have the miner convicted of assaulting an officer of the law. Alec allowed himself a smile of satisfaction as the judge sentenced the former miner to several years of hard labour.

The start of K.J. Anderson's trial was a big news day for Lucasville. Alec and all three of his deputies were called upon as witnesses to different parts of the case. Sam Liston hobbled into the court, looking infuriatingly dashing, in spite of his limp. He'd found himself an ebony cane with an ivory handle that he made a great show of using. Ethan didn't look as dramatic, but he was clear and solid as a witness, his face patently sincere. Alec couldn't help feeling a twinge of envy at Karl, coolly handsome and well spoken. He knew of the warmth and humour that lay under the aristocratic surface, but couldn't help wishing that he had something of Karl's inherent nobility, instead of being a short, dark-haired, displaced Scotsman.

When he was called forward to the witness box, Alec got his first chance to look back at the crowded public seats. His heart lifted as he saw Eileen Wessex, dressed charmingly in dusty pink. She smiled at him, and after a startled moment, Alec smiled back. He forgot his mild envy of his more dashing friends, and began his evidence in a clear voice.

At the end of that first day of the trial, Alec left the courthouse with his friends, to find Eileen waiting outside for him, along with a cluster of other people. He wanted to speak to Eileen, but some newspapermen pushed their way in closer, demanding more details of the case, especially the adventure on the train. Alec started at the flare of a magnesium camera flash going off close to his face. Alec managed to resist the temptation to growl at the reporters, and instead told them that he couldn't speak freely until the case was finished.

'Iffen you-all want photographs, you can take mine,' Sam suggested, striking a noble pose. 'I can tell you all about how our brave sheriff here stopped the train from running off the rails and plunging into the canyon below.'

The reporters began to turn his way, sensing they would get more from him than from the sheriff. Alec smothered a grin as Sam began to limp away, taking a trail of newspapermen with him. Sam was loving the attention, and at the same time freeing Alec from their questions.

After greeting Eileen, Karl announced firmly that he and the others would meet Alec back at the sheriff's office, and he left, taking Ethan along with him. Alec found himself alone with Eileen, smiling nervously at her.

'I thought you would have been in school today,' he remarked.

'It's the summer recess,' she told him. 'I have plenty of free time to do as I wish.'

'Then I would have thought that you could find something more interesting than attending a court case,' Alec said.

'And miss seeing the Hero Sheriff of Dereham County giving his evidence live in court?' she teased, quoting from the *Trumpet*.

Alec grimaced. 'I've been hearing that all week from Sam.'

'You deserve it,' Eileen said, no longer teasing. 'This county can be truly proud of its sheriff.'

'And his deputies,' Alec added. 'I couldna done without them.'

'You get the deputies you deserve,' Eileen said.

Alec laughed suddenly. 'When Sam's making me mad, I often wonder what I did to deserve him.'

Eileen smiled, and they simply stood at looked at one

another for a minute.

'You saved the lives of everyone on that train,' Eileen said at last.

Alec shrugged. 'I've driven a train a wee bit before. I knew what I needed to do.'

'And you did it. Some men wouldn't have kept their heads.'

'It's the way I am. My friends were depending on me.' Alec paused. 'I shouldn't like to live through that again, but before Donegan attacked, I remember thinking how lovely that country is. That's what I have to remember about it.'

'I looked at the sketches in the newspaper,' Eileen said. 'It's hard to believe anything so terrible could happen somewhere so beautiful.'

'Aye, it is beautiful,' Alec agreed. Taking a deep breath, he mustered his courage and said. 'I'd sure like to take ye to see it sometime.'

Eileen's brown eyes widened, making Alec panic, then her face widened into a lovely smile.

'I'd like to go with you, Alec.'

He broke into a wide grin. 'I'll hire a wee buggy and horse and show ye the mountains. It'll hafta be after this trial, mind,' he added.

'I don't mind waiting,' Eileen reassured him. 'The mountains won't go away in a matter of weeks.'

Alec nodded. 'I promise you I'll make the time.'

Eileen looked steadily at him, her eyes warm. 'And I know you're a man of your word.'

Alec just smiled.